'Hey, are you going to get out of this car?'

No! Meg wanted to scream. Not till next Christmas. Sam still hadn't noticed she was the size of a whale. There was still a chance to escape.

In her dreams!

Reaching over, she picked up her purse and two grocery bags from the passenger seat, shoved her squeaky door open, and stood with her packages hiding her stomach. She began the slow journey around the front of her car, avoiding meeting his eyes. She didn't want to see his face when he first recognised her condition.

But when she reached Sam and he didn't speak for the longest time, she was forced to look up.

And she knew as soon as she did that, to the end of her days, she would never forget the expression on his face.

'Meg!'

Barbara Hannay was born in Sydney, educated in Brisbane and has spent most of her adult life living in tropical North Queensland, where she and her husband have raised four children. While she has enjoyed many happy times camping and canoeing in the bush, she also delights in an urban lifestyle—chamber music, contemporary dance, movies and dining out. An English teacher, she has always loved writing, and now, by having her stories published, she is living her most cherished fantasy.

Recent titles by the same author:

OUTBACK WITH THE BOSS
OUTBACK BABY
HUSBANDS OF THE OUTBACK—with **Margaret Way**

THE PREGNANCY DISCOVERY

BY
BARBARA HANNAY

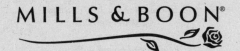

MILLS & BOON®

For Magnetic Island and my fortunate friends who live there.

First published in Great Britain 2001
Harlequin Mills & Boon Limited,
Eton House, 18-24 Paradise Road, Richmond, Surrey TW9 1SR

© Barbara Hannay 2001

ISBN 0 263 82610 4

Set in Times Roman 10½ on 12 pt.
02-0801-46970

Printed and bound in Spain
by Litografia Rosés, S.A., Barcelona

PROLOGUE

MEG almost missed seeing the old bottle lying half in, half out of the damp sand.

Most evenings, on her solitary walks along the beach on Magnetic Island, she found a trail of shells, broken coral and driftwood. She often came across fishing floats, pieces of timber from wrecks on the Great Barrier Reef…and bottles.

But this evening, just as she passed this particular bottle, a ray from the setting sun struck its glass. It glinted and winked at her. Meg paused and bent closer. It was then she noticed that the neck was sealed and a little stirring of curiosity, a prickle of anticipation, prompted her to reach down and tug the bottle out of its sandy bed.

At first she thought it was empty. But when she held it up to the fading light, she saw a shadowy cylinder of paper inside and her breath snagged on a sudden gasp.

A letter.

A letter in a bottle.

Her first reaction was excitement, a kind of childish thrill…and hot on its heels came a thousand questions. But then a strange kind of sixth sense buzzed through Meg.

Her heart drummed.

Shivering, she tried to shrug off the unsettling notion that she and the bottle shared a connection—a tenuous, but important link.

The feeling wouldn't go away.

Around her the tropical night was closing in. All that

was left of the sun was a blush of pink along the tops of the island's hills. The darkening waters of the bay threw themselves gently against the coral sand in a slow slap...slap...slap.

The rest of the world was going about its business, just as it did every evening, but Meg felt different...as if her life had been touched by an unseen hand.

Clutching the bottle to her chest, she hurried back up the beach and along the bush track to the car park. Carefully, she wrapped it in a towel and settled it safely under the passenger's seat of her Mini Moke. She would wait till she got back to her bungalow to open the bottle with great care and she would read its contents in complete privacy.

And then she would know...

CHAPTER ONE

THE last thing Sam Kirby needed was another pretty woman in his life.

His personal assistant, who spent her days juggling his crowded social calendar with his hectic business appointments, had told him so on many occasions.

So when he rushed into his downtown Seattle office straight from his latest corporate battle, he didn't expect to find a photo of a beautiful, bikini-clad girl smack on top of the paperwork needing his immediate attention.

'Ellen, what's this?' He spun around so abruptly he almost collided with his assistant, who'd been following faithfully at his heels.

Her eyes flicked anxiously to the photo. 'It came this morning in a courier express package from Australia.' She picked up several sheets from his desk. 'The operator of an island holiday resort sent it along with a news clipping and a letter.'

He frowned. 'If it's just an advertising gimmick, throw it in the bin. The way things are at present I won't be free to take a holiday any time in the next decade.'

'It's not advertising, Sam. I'm afraid there's more to it.'

With a grimace of exasperation, he took the clipping Ellen held out. The photo showed a lovely blonde standing on a postcard-perfect, tropical beach. Her name, the caption claimed, was Meg Bennet and she was holding an old bottle.

For a little longer than was strictly necessary, he let his gaze linger on her.

She wore a bikini top and a simple sarong in different shades of blue tied loosely around her slim hips. Her midriff glowed honey-gold and her hair was a pleasing tumble of sunshiny curls.

But she wasn't just another remarkably pretty girl.

What Sam found unexpectedly interesting, almost magnetic, was the disturbing directness of her smiling eyes as they looked straight out of the page at him.

It bugged him that he couldn't determine the exact colour of those eyes but, for a heady moment, he thought how interesting it would be to see them close up—just before he kissed her.

'Sam, your social diary is fully-booked well into next month,' his long suffering assistant remarked dryly, 'and that particular young woman lives on the other side of the Pacific.'

'Too bad,' he responded with a quick grin and a shrug before he refocused his concentration on the clipping from an Australian newspaper. 'Love letter found in bottle on tropical island,' he read aloud and, letting out an impatient sigh, he silently skimmed the rest of the story.

When he finished, he looked at Ellen with a puzzled frown. 'I don't understand why we've been sent this. Some American airman wrote a love letter to his bride back in 1942 and stuck it in a bottle and now it's turned up on the Great Barrier Reef almost sixty years later. So what?'

'Perhaps you were too side-tracked by the photo to notice,' Ellen prompted. 'But the story also mentions that they're trying to trace the American who wrote the letter, or his descendants.'

'But what has that to do with us at Kirby & Son?'

Ellen straightened her impeccably neat suit jacket.

And Sam felt a nasty jab of alarm. 'Ellen, what is it?'

She smiled gently. 'According to this letter from the manager of the island resort, the man who wrote the message in the bottle has been identified and his descendants have been traced.'

'And?'

'And his name was Thomas Jefferson Kirby—'

'My grandfather,' Sam completed in a choked, disbelieving whisper.

'Yes.'

'Whew!' He closed his eyes for a second or two. Slowly, he looked at Ellen again and shook his head. 'Tom Kirby died during the war. My father never even knew the poor guy.'

Again he stared at the photo and the bottle in the girl's hand. 'Who would have thought?' He held out his hand for the letter. 'What else does this Australian have to say?'

As he read, his stomach tightened an extra notch. 'What's he playing at? He reckons there was a new will in the bottle and he won't release the details until someone from my family goes over there.'

'There's no way your father could undertake that kind of journey.'

'Of course he can't, he's far too frail, but how the heck does this guy expect me to just drop everything and head off to some tropical island down under?' Groaning, he clapped a hand to his forehead. 'I don't have time to deal with this.'

Ellen looked at her young boss over her half glasses. 'There's a lot at stake. Kirby & Son has been in your family for four generations.'

'I know. I know.' Sam pushed aside thoughts of what

such stress might do to his ailing father. 'There's something suspicious about this Aussie. I don't like the way he's refusing to hand over the letter unless I show up in person.' With one hand rubbing his jaw, he added, 'I'll have to give this some thought.'

Ellen nodded and returned without comment to her desk in the adjoining office.

Tossing the photo and the papers onto his desk, Sam shoved his hands deep in his trouser pockets and strode towards the huge plate-glass window that overlooked the Seattle waterfront and the Bell Street Pier.

This sudden news about his grandfather had caught him way off-base.

It was the last thing he needed. Since his father's heart attack, Sam had sole responsibility for running the family's huge multimillion dollar construction company. He'd been working at a killing pace for the past three years and there was no sign of things slowing down.

Now, he'd been pitched a curve ball by an ancestor he'd rarely thought about and had never even mourned. He drew in an huge breath and let it out slowly, trying to diffuse the overwhelming sense of pressure.

Gloomily, he stared through the window at the world outside. From his vantage point, the whole of Seattle seemed stripped of any colour this afternoon. Although it was late spring, grey skies, and grey office blocks overlooked a grey waterfront. Even the offshore islands were dark charcoal smudges floating on dull slate-coloured water.

The idea of escape—especially of escaping to sunshine and warmth—had distinct appeal. He could collect this letter, steal a few days to dive on the coral reefs and smell the frangipani. Check out the colour of Meg Bennet's eyes...

Pacing the carpet back to his desk, his mind tussled with his dilemma. What he needed to know was whether this new will in Australia was genuine. If any of his competitors got wind of a will that could question the legal ownership of Kirby & Son, it would be like having an ace up their sleeves in a multimillion-dollar card game.

A discreet cough from the doorway interrupted his thoughts. 'Sam.' Ellen sounded hesitant, looked sympathetic. 'I just had a phone call from a reporter at the Seattle Times. He wants to talk to you. It seems the media already know about the bottle.'

Sam cursed under his breath.

'The press will make a field day out of it,' Ellen agreed. 'Especially after that society columnist dubbed you Seattle's favourite bachelor last week.'

He thrust an irate hand through his thick dark hair. 'I think I'm fast running out of options. I'll have to go to Australia and get this bottle business sorted out as quickly as possible.'

Ellen nodded. 'I can start making bookings.'

'Yeah, thanks. And I want my lawyers alerted to have someone on call round the clock—just in case this guy tries any tricks about my grandfather's will.' Sam paused and looked thoughtfully at the photo of the girl with the bottle.

Ellen followed his gaze and she sighed. 'Poor Meg Bennet.'

'Why do you say that?'

'She looks rather sweet. I can't help thinking that if you're planning to zip over to her quiet little island for a few days and zap straight back here again, you should be wearing hazard lights.'

Sam frowned and looked affronted. 'I'm not a danger to women. I'm just attracted to them.'

'Of course,' Ellen replied, but she walked away muttering something about charm having its own perils and wouldn't it be fitting if the tables were turned one of these days.

His glance flicked to the picture of the intriguing Meg Bennet. There was a spunky intelligence and honesty about her lovely face that suggested she wouldn't let any man get the better of her unless she wanted him to.

But he quickly dismissed such thoughts. It was the will, his grandfather's message in the bottle, that he was going to Australia to pick up. Not the beautiful girl who'd happened to find it.

Meg was pleased. The reef was looking its best this morning. As she snorkelled back towards the shallows of Florence Bay, no breath of wind stirred the surface of the pleasantly warm water, and the sun shone from a cloudless sky. The underwater visibility was perfect for her group of tourists to view the spectacular fantasy below.

Beneath them now, copper and gold butterfly-fish with elongated snouts were probing vibrant red coral clumps. Nearby, forests of branching staghorn coral, bright blue with deep pink tips, shimmered, pretty as Christmas trees.

A spotted ray, camouflaged on the sea bed, suddenly exploded in a cloud of white sand, the tips of its flat body rippling as it arched away.

All morning, she'd been guiding the resort's guests through a treasure trove of natural beauty. She always got a kick out of sharing the excitement of first timers when they discovered the incredible secrets of the tropical sea.

Reaching the shallows, she stood and balanced first on one foot and then the other, as she pulled off her flippers.

Then she removed her snorkel and mask and waited for the holiday makers she'd been escorting to join her.

The American, who was closest to her, ripped off his face mask and exclaimed, 'That was just fantastic. I never expected to see so many varieties of damselfish in the one spot.'

'So you know about damselfish? Sounds like you did some research before you came on holiday,' Meg suggested as they waded towards the crescent of sand that fringed the bay.

'I haven't had any time for research recently, but I've been interested in tropical fish since I was so high.' He gestured somewhere near his knee and grinned.

Oh, boy! Meg gulped as the full impact of that grin hit her. This man's smile outranked the big screen efforts of most movie stars.

And his eyes were an unexpected drowsy blue. She was perturbed by the way that just looking at him made her breathing quicken, dislodging the comfortable friendliness she usually shared with resort guests.

Dropping her snorkelling gear onto the sand, she reached for her towel and made a business of squeezing excess moisture from her hair. What was the matter with her? This American wasn't the first handsome tourist she'd taken skin-diving.

She promised herself that a reaction like that wouldn't happen again. This fellow could smile as much as he liked and she would remain immune. She'd seen one or two of her workmates get themselves into dreadful emotional pickles, breaking their hearts over resort guests. It just wasn't worth it.

Waving to the group of German tourists, who were making their way out of the water, she decided that it must be this blue-eyed boy's excitement about the reef that gave him an extra edge of attractiveness.

But she felt ridiculously self-conscious about unzipping the full-length Lycra bodysuit she'd worn as protection from marine stingers.

Her companion didn't hesitate to shed his suit and Meg found herself stealing a peek at the tall, wide-shouldered and tautly muscled body that emerged clad in simple bathers. She had no alternative but to step out of her suit, too. Nevertheless, she avoided his gaze.

It was very annoying that she should suddenly feel so bothered about something she did every day.

When they both hauled on T-shirts, she felt better, but there was still a self-conscious edge to her voice when she said, 'We'll head back to the resort now. You'll have time for a shower before lunch.'

The Germans, who had their own hired vehicles, were talking animatedly amongst themselves and so the American helped Meg to pile the snorkelling equipment into the back of the resort's Mini Moke and he sent her another breath-robbing grin. 'Thanks for a great morning.'

'My pleasure,' she murmured.

They both jumped into her Moke and, as she steered the little vehicle up the winding track leading out of the bay, her passenger leaned comfortably back in his seat, turned to her and asked, 'OK Miss Recreation Officer, what's planned for this afternoon?'

Surprised, she shot him a calculating glance, but smiled as she said, 'You Americans are so energetic when you come on holidays, aren't you? It's go, go, go the whole time.'

His eyebrows rose. 'That's so unusual?'

'I don't suppose so,' she admitted. 'But we don't have

a huge number of guests here at the moment and most of them seem to be fairly independent, so I didn't have anything organised for this afternoon.'

'I was hoping you might be able to take me on a guided tour of one of the island's walks.'

Meg pursed her lips. Was this fellow making a play for her already? When she'd come to work at the resort just three months ago, she'd discovered that far too many male visitors arrived on the island and assumed the female staff were part of the room service along with the free tea and coffee. She'd developed some pretty useful brush-off tactics.

'If you have a look in that glove box, you'll find a pamphlet that outlines all the walks. You're a big boy. You don't need a guide. Anyhow…' she added a white lie as an extra measure of protection '…I'm busy all afternoon. There's a VIP coming soon.'

'Big deal is it?'

'Oh, just some hotshot millionaire.' Meg rolled her eyes.

'You don't think much of millionaires?'

Her scowl was automatic. Five years ago, she'd watched her father's career and health suffer at the hands of a money-hungry tycoon and she'd developed a seriously jaundiced view of wealth. 'I'm sure those types are so busy counting their money, or protecting it, or making it grow, they don't have time for the important things in life.'

'I'm sure you're right,' he said in a strangely flat voice that made Meg look at him sharply.

They crested the hill and in front of them stretched a magnificent vista—a string of pretty blue bays sparkling in the midday sun like sapphires on a necklace.

As the American admired the view, he said casually,

'I heard something about a bottle being found on one of those beaches.'

'Yes.' A sudden sprinkling of goose bumps broke out on Meg's arms. 'I found it,' she told him.

Sam's guilty conscience gave him a bad time as he watched Meg's face grow wistful. He should come clean and confess to her that he was the very millionaire she had been talking about. He should tell her right now.

But an equally strong instinct urged him otherwise. She was already wary of him and a confession like that would make her clam up completely. Then he would miss this heaven-sent opportunity to pick up inside information about the bottle and its message before he tackled her boss.

They reached the resort, Magnetic Rendezvous. She steered the car into a parking bay and, after turning the engine off, leaned forward, linking her arms across the top of the steering wheel. Sam got the distinct impression she was pleased to talk to someone about this bottle.

She turned to look at him and he felt the full impact of her clear grey eyes. Yes, they were definitely grey, he decided—and sweetly framed by long dark lashes. And, he noticed uncomfortably, right now they were shimmering with a suspicious sheen.

'I don't know what made me pick the bottle up,' she said softly. 'I keep asking myself that and I know it sounds fanciful, but it was almost as if I was *meant* to find it.'

Her face softened into a sad, dreamy smile and Sam felt a surprising constriction in his throat. In the flesh, Meg was even lovelier than her photo had suggested. The photo hadn't shown the way she moved, light and grace-ful, with a sexy little sway of her hips. It couldn't record the delightful warmth of her voice or capture the way her smile could dissolve into a sweetly serious frown when she was lost in thought.

She was looking serious now when she said, 'That bottle spent sixty years bobbing around in the ocean. I'm only—well—it's more than twice my age.'

'So how old does that make you?'

'None of your business.'

Sam grinned. At a guess, he'd put her age at around twenty-four or twenty-five. He was thirty-two, so she was a bit young for him—not that he was thinking of her in that way, of course.

Then again…

She was offering him a view of her delicate profile and, as he watched the way she nibbled at her soft bottom lip, a guy couldn't help contemplating how nice it would be to try that himself sometime.

Meg's voice broke into his thoughts, dragging them away from highly unsuitable fantasies. 'I guess I'm looking at this whole bottle business in a hopelessly romantic way.' She flashed him a sudden smile.

He couldn't resist smiling back. 'What's wrong with romance?'

For a long moment their gazes held. An unspoken, highly charged exchange flashed between them. Sam only just resisted an urge to lean forward and taste her soft, startled mouth.

He couldn't be sure who looked away first but, eventually, they both stared back out through the windscreen at the stretch of lawn dotted with coconut palms.

He forced himself to remember that his family's business was at stake. Which was why he was relaxing on a tropical island and deliberately misleading this lovely young woman. He definitely shouldn't be planning to add seduction to his crime of deception.

He cleared his throat. 'So this message in the bottle, was it a love letter?'

She nodded. 'It's beautiful. That man sure loved the woman he was writing to.'

'He was writing to his wife, wasn't he?'

'Yes, but you can't read her name. There's some damage—from exposure to light we think.'

He repressed an angry sigh. If Tom Kirby's wife wasn't naméd, sorting out this will could be really messy. It was the worst possible news.

'You'd better not ask me any more about it,' Meg said with sudden briskness, 'I can't say anything else, not when the grandson of Thomas Kirby, the man who wrote the message, is coming here soon—tomorrow, I think.'

Sam's stomach tightened guiltily.

Meg added, 'He's the American VIP I was telling you about.'

'You don't say?' he murmured, and he switched his attention to a rainbow lorikeet as it settled in a nearby tree. After promising himself, *again,* to come clean very soon, he asked, 'So this guy is coming all the way out here just to pick up a sixty-year-old letter? Why couldn't you have posted it to him special delivery?'

Meg sighed loudly. 'That would be too easy. My boss wouldn't hear of it. He wants to get as much publicity mileage as he can out of this incident.'

He stopped studying the bird and turned to frown at her. 'What kind of publicity?'

'He sees this as a great opportunity to get media attention for the resort. Magnetic Rendezvous isn't doing all that well. The competition for the tourist dollar is very stiff.'

So that was what this guy was after! 'That's cheeky.'

'Oh, Fred's cheeky all right. He wants shots of me and

this bachelor millionaire with the bottle plastered in newspapers and on television screens all over the country. I'm not looking forward to it,' she said with another sigh.

'This man—this millionaire—'

'Yes?'

'He might—' Sam hesitated, uncomfortably aware that if he kept on talking about himself, he was taking this whole subterfuge thing way too far.

To his relief, Meg didn't wait for him to finish. She jumped out of the doorless Moke and grinned at him. 'I prefer not to think about him until I have to. Now, you're going to miss out on lunch if you don't get moving.'

He hopped out of the car too, and strode around to the back where she had begun to sort out the tangle of snorkels and flippers. 'There's something I should explain.'

'What's that?'

His eyes rested her. Her beauty was as fresh and natural, as untouched as the island itself. *Tell her,* an inner voice urged and he drew in a breath, ready to confess. 'There's something I should tell you…something I should get off my chest about why I'm here on the island.'

Meg stopped counting flippers and looked up abruptly to frown at him. 'Now you really have me intrigued.' She touched his wrist lightly. 'You'll have to explain…*Heavens!* I've been rattling on to you and I can't even remember your name. What did you say your name was again?'

'Sam.'

'OK, Sam.' Her grey eyes looked directly into his. 'Get it off your chest.'

Her gaze suddenly locked with his and, just as he had

earlier, Sam felt another startling sense of connection zap between them.

Her warm hand was still lying on his wrist.

Neither of them moved.

Chemistry could play sneaky tricks on a guy. Sam would have liked to feel more in control of this situation. Getting to know a woman was usually a pleasant game where he called all the shots. Many considered him to be an expert.

But right now, he had no idea where he was heading.

Especially when, out of absolutely nowhere, the unmistakable idea of kissing hovered between them in the dappled sunlight.

As if prompted by a magnetic force, he dipped his head towards Meg ever so slightly and, to his surprise, she didn't pull back. When he leaned lower, she raised her face a breathless fraction higher.

Their mouths met.

It was a hello kind of kiss. More than friendly, but not exactly the exchange of lovers. Apart from their mouths and her hand on his, they weren't touching. He smiled down at her and she smiled back and he felt the warmth and softness of her linger on his lips and the blood rush through his pulse points.

Meg was looking at him in dazed alarm as if she was as startled as he was. Then she jumped back, glaring at him and she said shakily, 'I make it a rule never to kiss guests.'

The flustered, breathless way she spoke sounded so sexy Sam stepped back too, in case he gave in to any more urges. 'I won't tell anyone.'

She grabbed a pile of flippers, as if she needed an armful of rubber to keep him at bay. 'You said you wanted to tell me something important about why you're here,' she reminded him sharply. 'What sort of work did you say you did?'

'Er—don't worry about my job. It's boring,' Sam replied hastily. 'But my hobby is marine science. I haven't studied it in depth, but I'd love to learn more about the life on the reef, underwater photography, salt-water aquariums—that sort of thing. We could make a great team. You could be my tutor.'

'Bad idea.' She scowled. And then, like a mother scolding a little boy, she added, 'I suggest you go take a shower and have some lunch.'

She looked so mad that any thought of confessing his identity seemed ridiculous now. But it also seemed important to set things straight with Meg. For some inexplicable reason, Sam really cared what she thought of him.

A flipper dropped from the pile she was clutching and landed at his feet. He picked it up and held it for a moment, his fingers flexing the rubber. 'Meg, what I meant to tell you was that this VIP you mentioned...'

He could sense her wariness, as if she'd pulled it on like protective armour. From beneath ash-blonde curls streaked with gold, her grey gaze darkened to a stormy charcoal. 'Don't tell me it's you,' she whispered.

'Yeah, 'fraid so.'

A red flush flared in her cheeks and he couldn't tell if she was embarrassed or just plain mad at him.

'I'm sorry. I meant to tell you earlier.'

'No one was stopping you,' she snapped.

'Maybe not, but I didn't see why I should give you a perfect reason to hate me.'

'Yes, but—' Meg gulped.

'And you handed me an excellent opportunity to check out the lie of the land. I don't intend to just waltz in to your boss ready to dance to his tune. After all, there's a lot at stake.'

'A lot of money.'

'More than just money. It's complicated.' He took a step closer and offered her what he hoped was a reassuring smile. 'But I have an even better excuse.'

Meg didn't smile back. She continued to stand stiffly to attention with her arms tightly wrapped around the flippers.

'I really appreciated being able to see the reef just the way I did this morning—just like an ordinary tourist. I had a great time. Thank you. From what you've said, the media will be hanging around tomorrow. Things will be different.' He smiled again.

But it seemed the effort was wasted.

Meg's chin lifted and she eyed him with a haughty glare. 'Things will be very different,' she said. 'For starters, you won't even *think* about trying to kiss me.'

He tucked the flipper into the bundle she was holding. 'In that case, I'm sure neither of us will look forward to tomorrow.'

Ignoring her startled gasp, he turned in the direction of his bungalow. And, as he walked away, Sam reflected that he'd been wise not to add a comment about just how slim Meg's chances were if she expected to control his thoughts.

Especially his thoughts about kissing her again.

CHAPTER TWO

As soon as she woke the next morning, Meg knew it was going to be a bad day. Her first clue was the way her mind flashed straight to Sam Kirby—exactly where she didn't want it to be. He'd taken up far too much space in her head all night.

Not even the rainbow lorrikeets that came to her kitchen window for their breakfast treat could lift her spirits. She watched the amazing birds peck daintily at tiny pieces of bread and honey. But this morning their bright purple heads, lime-green wings, and bright yellow chests, brush-stroked with scarlet, didn't fill her with admiration as they usually did. She was too busy feeling angry.

The cheek of the man—hiding his identity, encouraging her to talk about the bottle and then stealing that kiss—all in such a short space of time!

If ever a man spelled danger for Meg, Sam Kirby did. He was a super-rich big businessman and an international resort guest—he summed up everything she went out of her way to avoid. So how on earth had she stood there like a ninny and let him kiss her?

And the worst part was, it had been such a nice kiss.

Despite her anger, she'd found herself thinking about it over and over as she'd drifted off to sleep. Again and again, she'd remembered the warm, sensual pressure of his slightly open lips on hers. Then there was the impact of those deep blue eyes up close. They had been breathtaking. They'd made her think about...finding somewhere private...somewhere beneath whispering palm trees...or in the shallows on a secluded sandy beach...somewhere...anywhere he could go on kissing her...

But, for heaven's sake! These were things she most certainly shouldn't be thinking about on first meeting a man. Especially *this* man. She'd spent the rest of the night telling herself that.

Remember who he is. A corporate high roller.

A playboy millionaire. Forget him!

He'll be gone in a few days. Forget him, now!

The fact that he'd come to the island to collect the letter in the bottle was a snag. She'd already agreed to her boss's demands to pose with Sam for the publicity shots today, so she had little choice now, but to eat her breakfast, shower and get ready for the ordeal.

But, as she did so, Meg kept up a continuous pep talk in her head. By the time she left her bungalow, she was determined to be mentally prepared to face Sam again.

A swarm of journalists, television cameramen and photographers hovered around the reception area. When Meg arrived, some were pacing the slate tiles, while others settled back on the deep cane lounges to smoke and chat quietly.

Her boss, Fred Raynor, dragged her excitedly into his office. 'I was about to have you paged. All the media have turned up! They came over on the early boat. Isn't this great?'

He beamed and rubbed his pudgy hands together. 'And these are just the local press. When their stories get out, there'll be more.' He flung a hand to the view of the resort's tropical garden. 'It's going to be a beautiful day in paradise. We'll get excellent outdoor shots.'

'All we need is our millionaire,' Meg added dryly.

'He'll be here any minute.' Fred shook his head and ran a hand over his bulging stomach. 'Boy, did that guy upset my digestion last night.'

'Oh?' Meg couldn't help being curious.

'He wanted the letter out of the bottle straight away and was wild as a cut snake when I said he could only have it after he posed for a few photos.'

'Did he refuse to go ahead with the publicity?' she asked hopefully.

'I finally got him to agree. I told him flat I've got possession. He can carry on about his lawyers and rights, but down here it's finders keepers.' Fred's pale eyes gleamed as he looked at her meaningfully. 'Actually, I think what won him round was the fact that it gives him a good excuse to hang around—er, *here*—for a day or two.'

He looked over Meg's shoulder as someone entered the office and he lowered his voice. 'Here he is now.'

Standing stiffly to attention, Meg clenched her hands into tight little fists at her sides as she turned to face Sam.

'Morning,' he said with his usual smile.

'It's going to be good one.' Fred beamed.

'Hello, Meg,' Sam added when she didn't respond. His eyes held a twinkling warmth.

Meg nodded frostily. 'Hi.' She found herself needing to search for outward signs of wealth on Sam Kirby— things she might have overlooked yesterday—when she'd been taken up with his *other* attributes.

His watch was a sophisticated diving watch, but many men wore similar accessories. His dark blue, open-necked shirt, stone-coloured shorts and navy trainers were probably expensive, but spoke of taste rather than money. There was no hint of jewellery around his neck, at his wrist, or on his fingers.

So he wasn't flashy. That still didn't mean she could trust him.

Fred slapped them both on the shoulder and grinned broadly. 'Let's get this show on the road.'

Feeling annoyingly self-conscious again, Meg followed the men out of the office. As she expected, Fred wanted plenty of publicity shots set up in front of the huge Magnetic Rendezvous sign. She was required to pose with Sam.

'Smile into each other's eyes now,' a photographer called.

Meg tried to force a smile and focused on a point beyond Sam's shoulder. She knew he was looking straight at her, smiling with those baby-blue, super-cute eyes, but she was determined not to let them affect her again.

'Hey, miss, lighten up,' a photographer scolded.

She squeezed her smile muscles harder as Sam leaned closer.

'They're blue today.' His voice was a sexy rumble close to her ear.

Goose bumps prickled to unwilling life on her arms. Her gaze lifted to meet his. *Gulp*. No matter how she felt about him, Sam was still the best-looking guy she'd seen outside a cinema. 'What are blue? What are you talking about?'

'Your eyes,' he said softly. 'How do they do it?'

'Do what?' she muttered through her grimacing smile.

'Change colour. I've been trying to work out what colour they are and yesterday I decided they were definitely grey, but today I swear they're blue.'

Meg couldn't help it. She smiled.

Cameras flashed all around them. 'That's great!' someone shouted. 'Hold that smile! Gorgeous!' There were more flashes and clicks.

As a photographer rearranged them into a slightly different pose, Sam asked, 'How do they change like that?'

He was doing it again. Trying to win her over with charm. Most men usually focused their attention somewhere between her neck and her knees. No man, in her memory, had ever paid such flattering attention to her eyes.

'Does their colour depend on what you're wearing?' His approving gaze took in her aqua halter-necked top and shorts.

'I think so.'

'That's a really neat trick.'

But Meg was determined not to be won over by a few throw-away lines about her eyes.

Suddenly a female journalist in a trendy power suit stepped forward wielding a microphone. A cameraman and sound recorder crowded close behind.

'Mr Kirby,' the journalist asked silkily. 'I understand you've dated film stars and celebrities in America? So what do you think of Australian girls?'

Meg made a choking sound. Where on earth had this stupid question come from? What did it have to do with the letter in the bottle? Didn't the ditsy journalist know about sticking to the hard facts?

Sam looked a little startled by the question, too, but he quickly recovered. He favoured the journalist with a full-scale model of his sexiest smile. 'Aussie girls are enchanting.'

The journalist simpered and Meg might have scowled if the camera hadn't swung to focus on her. The interviewer spoke again, 'And, Meg, what's it like to have the attention of Seattle's favourite bachelor?'

'It's been an enlightening experience,' she replied coolly.

The journalist's eyebrow arched. 'Can you tell us exactly how you've been enlightened?'

Meg smiled slowly. 'No.'

Taken aback, the journalist stared at Meg for several long seconds before trying Sam again. 'We're told that this story isn't just about a romance that happened sixty years ago.' Her eyes slid meaningfully from Meg to Sam. 'I understand there's a little chemistry happening right now?'

Meg glared over her shoulder at her boss, who was slinking behind a clump of golden cane palms. She heard the angry hiss of Sam's breath. When she glanced his way, she saw that his smile had been replaced by a displeased, stony stare.

'You heard Miss Bennet,' he said. 'No comment.'

The journalist shrugged and rolled her eyes.

To Meg's relief, someone else called, 'OK, now we'll take some beach shots! Everyone down at the water's edge.'

On the beach, the morning sun hung above them, a dazzling white-gold blaze in the sky. Beneath it, the bay stretched like a shimmering sheet of liquid gold.

A cameraman hurried to set up his tripod.

And a bottle was thrust into Sam's hands. 'This is *it*? This is *the* bottle?' He turned to Meg.

She nodded.

The bottle was empty and Meg stood quietly as he examined the ancient, once clear, green glass carefully, turning it over and over, slowly. He seemed to be studying the surface, which was worn to an opaque haze by sand and salt and endless, endless water.

Her mouth quivered into a funny little trembling smile as she watched him and she wondered if he felt as choked up as she did. This was the bottle that had been held by Tom Kirby, his grandfather. All those years ago.

For days now, she'd been thinking about this moment when it was handed over to its rightful owner. She looked at Sam through moist eyes. 'It's good to know you have it at last,' she said in a voice choked with emotion.

Once more, cameras clicked and whirred as photographers crouched and hovered around them. 'That's lovely, sweetheart.' *Click!* 'Keep looking at him like that.' *Click! Click!* 'Beautiful.'

As soon as there was a break, Sam's face pulled into a wry grimace as he looked at her. 'I'll be happier when I get the letter as well as this bottle.'

Meg stiffened. All he cared about was the letter and the will and securing his family's business. She should have known a playboy bachelor from Seattle wouldn't have a sentimental bone in his body.

'Now, put your arm around her, mate,' another voice instructed.

Before she could prepare herself, Sam's strong arm settled around Meg's shoulders. She was gathered against him and of course her curves fitted perfectly against the hard planes of his muscular physique. This close, she could smell his skin, clean with a hint of expensive aftershave…and annoying, undeniable ripples of awareness heated her.

This was way too close for comfort.

'Put your hand on the bottle, too,' someone instructed. 'That's it—both of you holding it together.'

'Now, look deep into each other's eyes.'

Reluctantly, Meg dragged her eyes up to meet Sam's. This wasn't fair! Her resistance was wearing off. Suddenly, looking into those blue depths was like taking off from a high diving board. Her foolish heart leapt in her chest.

She tried for a joke—anything to take her mind off her body's embarrassing reactions. 'I guess we can regard this as practice for when we get married.' Then she cringed. *Idiot! Had she really said that?* 'I mean married to—whoever we marry,' she stammered, suddenly terribly flustered. '*If* we get ever married.' *How did she get into this mess?* 'Either of us, that is—' she added, floundering hopelessly. 'Either of us get married to anyone,' she finished lamely.

Looking into Sam's sexy eyes had emptied her mind of all cohesive thoughts.

'I get the picture, Meg.' He smiled.

'Have I gone bright red?' she asked him, as the cameras clicked away.

'Just a very becoming pink.' His amused eyes looked deep into hers as he tugged her a little closer.

His lips were so temptingly close. Meg had the distinct impression that he would have liked to kiss her again. She felt her own lips part and a little tremor of anticipation danced across them.

Thank goodness for Fred and the photographers! She was safe from Sam's kisses while they were around. How could any part of her feeble brain be contemplating kissing this man hot on the heels of yesterday's fiasco? Today she was supposed to be working doubly hard at keeping Sam at bay.

To her relief, the photo session was over at last. Someone mentioned that the next ferry would arrive soon, and the media dispersed, scrambling to leave for another assignment.

Meg squinted at the sky, taking deep breaths to regain her equilibrium. 'Time to get out of the sun.'

'You have a busy schedule today?' Sam asked as they passed under criss-crossing fronds of coconut palms on the way back to the resort.

She wasn't going to fall for any more of his come-on lines. 'I'm exceedingly busy,' she answered emphatically. 'I have meetings...'

He nodded. 'But would you have dinner with me tonight?'

She pressed her lips tightly together. Not only did she have to ward off this man's charm, now she had to deal with his persistence as well.

Sam added softly, 'It can be my way of paying you back for the dirty hand I dealt you yesterday.'

Meg was proud of her crisp reply. 'You don't owe me anything.'

'I owe you a great deal.' He stopped walking and looked down at the bottle he was still holding. Then he tossed it lightly from one hand to the other. 'Whatever happens, my family will be grateful to you for my grandfather's letter.'

'Whatever happens?' Meg repeated. 'You sound like you're really worried about how this will turn out.'

His face tightened and he looked away at some spot down the beach. 'I'll feel a lot better when that will is safely in the hands of my lawyers.'

'You said there's a lot at stake.'

'Yeah.' His fingers toyed with the bottle's mouth. 'Meg—about my grandfather's letter—you've read it, haven't you?'

'Yes.'

'Can you tell me more about it? Are you sure there's no way of telling who it was addressed to?'

'No, I'm afraid not. As I told you, the top of the page was damaged.'

'And there was no other reference to his wife's name?'

'No. The rest of the time he referred to "my wife" or "darling" or "sweetheart"—that kind of thing.'

Sam sighed heavily. 'But there was definitely a will?'

'It definitely made mention of Tom leaving all his worldly goods to his wife.'

'Yeah, well, Fred had better hand it over soon.' He gripped the bottle tightly with both hands for a moment, then suddenly smiled at her.

If only he would stop doing that!

'Why don't you forgive me for yesterday? I hear there's a very good outdoor restaurant over in one of the other bays.'

Fighting back the wild urge to accept was like trying to put out a bushfire with a mere tumbler of water. For Pete's sake, Sam was by far the best-looking fellow who'd ever asked Meg out. But, she had to be sensible about this. He'd be gone in a day or two. She took in a deep breath and let it out slowly. 'Thanks for the invite, Sam, but I'll have to decline.'

Before she changed her mind, she turned and walked quickly away.

Sam watched her go, a wry, admiring smile tugging his lips. When she'd rejected his invitation, she hadn't added, *I can't trust you,* but that was what she'd meant.

Of course, he couldn't blame Meg for running. He'd given her every reason to be wary. Yesterday, she'd been totally upfront and honest with him and he hadn't returned the compliment.

Her disdain was exactly what he deserved.

But Meg Bennet was having a strange effect on him. Just thinking about her…about her eyes…her hair…her mouth made him…*restless.* Was it because she was different? Because she refused to be impressed by the thing that impressed most women—his money? Because she refused to be impressed by *anything* about him?

His gaze dropped again to the bottle in his hands and he reminded himself that he hadn't come to Australia looking for romance. He had a business to run and he had to get back to it as soon as possible.

By tomorrow, he'd be grateful Meg had turned him down.

Meg dropped a peach-coloured bath bomb into the warm water and watched it explode and fizz. The steam in her bathroom began to distil a sensuous mixture of citrus and flowers. Dipping her big toe into the fragrant liquid, she felt her body begin at once to relax. She visualised submerging beneath the heated, scented surface of the water.

Br-ring! Br-ring!

Heavens, no! Not the telephone! Hovering with one leg in the air, she glared at the slim, cordless machine lying on the counter next to her hand basin. She toyed with the notion of letting it ring. But, officially, she was still on duty. With an impatient sigh, she crossed the room and picked it up but, as she answered, she returned with it to the bath. There was no way she would waste that beautifully scented hot water.

'Meg! It's Fred Raynor,' the voice snapped.

'Yes, Fred?' She lowered herself into the bath and felt the warm liquid swirl softly, seductively around her body. Fragrance drifted upwards, teasing her nostrils, enticing her to relax.

'You're not busy tonight are you?'

'Oh? Not particularly.' Meg grimaced and rolled her eyes to the ceiling. What on earth could her boss want now? Since she'd refused Sam's invitation to dinner, she'd had an ongoing battle with her weaker self all afternoon.

That was the main reason she needed to relax now. To pamper herself after a nerve-racking, miserable day.

'I want you to take Sam Kirby out to dinner, over at Alma Bay.'

Meg gulped. 'I have to?'

'Damn right you do.' Fred snapped.

Frowning, she sat up higher out of the water. She held the phone closer to her ear. 'Fred, you know this is way beyond the limits of my job as recreation officer.'

'But we need to keep this guy on our side. There's a good chance we can get national coverage out of this. He's big time. We could even get an international story if we play our cards right.'

'I'm sorry, Fred. I posed for your photos, but this is definitely going too far. It's verging on sexual harassment.'

She was relieved when, after a noisy grumble, her boss rang off.

Surprised that he'd given in so easily, Meg was about to drop the phone onto the bath mat when it rang again.

'Give up, Fred!' she cried. 'I am not going to dinner with Sam Kirby. Got it?'

'I'm reading you loud and clear.'

'Sam?' she demanded. 'Is that you?'

'It is,' came a response from the other end of the line.

'For Pete's sake, what do you want?' She knew it was ridiculous, but Meg scrambled over the edge of the bath to grab at a fluffy white towel. Even talking on the phone to Sam felt dangerous when she was naked. 'Did you get Fred to order me out to dinner with you?'

'I won't ruin my reputation by answering that.' There

was a pause and then he asked in a lighter tone, 'Did I hear splashing?'

'Er, I doubt it,' she muttered, wrapping herself in the huge towel and perching on the side of the bath.

'I'm sorry if I interrupted something.'

Meg wanted to be angry. She wanted to depress the disconnect button and to slip back beneath the warm and welcoming water. But the weak side of her clung to the phone, liking too much the sound of his deep voice with that musical North American twang. Besides, she was desperately curious. 'What did you want?'

'Actually, it *was* to try one more time to ask you to dinner, but without Fred's assistance. Hey, if you were taking a bath, go right ahead. Don't waste the water.'

'I might just do that.'

'By the way,' he continued, 'I have a very interesting scientific question.'

'Oh?'

'Are you near a mirror?'

'What do you think? I'm in a bathroom.'

'Could you look in the mirror for me and tell me what colour your eyes are when you're not wearing clothes?'

Instinctively, Meg's glance flashed to the mirror. But then her cheeks warmed. 'I'll tell you no such thing.' She flung her towel aside and slipped back into the bath.

There was an exaggerated sigh on the other end of the line. 'Another mystery of science remains unanswered.'

'I guess your eyes stay blue all the time,' she heard herself say and she wondered how that sultry, flirtatious little hum had crept into her voice.

'Yeah. I'm afraid my eyes are boring, boring.'

Hardly boring, Sam, she thought, but didn't dare say so. She lifted her feet out of the suds and rested her toes on the end of the bath, wondering if she should apply some nail polish to make them more glamorous and, the very next second, wondered why they needed to look glamorous.

'OK,' he added, 'try this. While you're soaking in the tub, practise saying, "Yes, Sam, I'd love to join you for dinner."'

To her amazement, Meg heard herself purring a reply in her very best attempt at an American accent. 'Yes, Sam, I'd *lurve* to join you for dinner.'

'Wonderful. I'll meet you at your place at seven.'

She nearly dropped the phone. 'Hold on! I was only copying your accent! That wasn't a real acceptance.'

'Oh, but Meg,' he replied, his voice warm and hinting somehow that he was smiling his hottest smile, 'it was a very, very real invitation.'

When he didn't hang up but waited in silence for her response, Meg closed her eyes and willed herself to be strong. She was furious with this man. She should have hung up as soon as she'd heard his voice.

Letting out her breath on a gusty sigh, she told him, 'Nice try, Sam Kirby but, as I said at the start, give up.'

'Now, that,' he replied in a husky baritone, 'is a distinct challenge. I can warn you now, Meg Bennet, if I set myself a goal, I *never* give up.'

'And what goal are you aiming for?'

There was a long pause and Meg thought she heard a faint chuckle. 'I'd settle for your acceptance of my apology. For yesterday.'

Meg closed her eyes. 'OK. Apology accepted,' she whispered.

'Good,' he said simply. 'And dinner?'

After a beat, she answered, 'Dinner declined.'

She disconnected the phone and let it drop onto the bath mat and, sinking beneath the sudsy water, she wished she felt more pleased about turning Sam down.

CHAPTER THREE

AS SHE ate her simple supper of cheese on toast, Meg tried not to think about what it would have been like to be dining with Sam. She kept reminding herself that he and the bottle would soon be going home to the United States and she was wise to stay well out of the way. How silly she'd been to imagine that somehow her own destiny was linked to that bottle.

The only connection she had was stumbling across it on the beach and giving way to natural curiosity.

Finishing her meal, she carried her plate through to the kitchen and decided she'd seen too much significance in finding the bottle. Perhaps she'd been grasping at straws. There was a good chance she'd been looking for anything that would help her out of the depressing loneliness she felt these days. Ever since her father had died just three months ago.

It had been bad enough giving up her postgraduate studies in marine biology to nurse her dad through the last horrible months of his illness. But nothing had prepared her for the bereft emptiness of her life after he'd died. He was all the family she'd had. Her mother had died when she was only little and her father had meant everything to her. Since his death, Meg thought she had discovered the utter depths of loneliness.

But tonight she felt more desolate than ever.

The sand crunched beneath Sam's shoes as he walked towards the water. By the light of a glowing white moon,

Florence Bay looked beautiful. On either side of the bay, dark rocky headlands curved out to protect the deserted beach. Hoop pines, rising majestically from between granite boulders, were silhouetted in inky black strokes against the gun metal sky.

The dark water lapped gently.

Somewhere out there in the wider ocean beyond the reefs, Tom Kirby lay at rest. Thinking about his grandfather and the bottle, he hunkered down on the sand and stared ahead. These past few years, he'd been working so hard he hadn't stopped to contemplate anything deep or meaningful—like death and the hereafter. Or life for that matter.

Lately, he'd been sensing an uneasy awareness that his own life was hurtling forward like a runaway train and he wasn't at all sure he was heading in the right direction. He was doing the right thing by his family—carrying on the Kirby tradition—and working damn hard to keep it successful—and playing hard, too, when time permitted. But he knew deep down that neither his work nor his play was really making him happy.

Lost in thought, he didn't hear footsteps so, when a voice suddenly sounded close behind him, he jumped to his feet.

'Sam, what are you doing here?'

'Meg!'

She was standing a metre or so away from him, her face pale and her eyes wide with surprise. She was wearing a soft blue sweater and white jeans and, in the moonlight, her hair had a silvery sheen and she looked breathtakingly lovely.

He turned and extended an arm towards the sea. 'It may sound a little weird, but I'm paying my respects.'

'To your grandfather?'

'Yeah.' Sam shoved his hands in his pockets to prevent himself from reaching for her. 'I rang my lawyers this afternoon. They've been doing some research for me and I couldn't believe what they told me.' He kicked at a knob of bleached coral lying on the sand. 'Tom Kirby died on this day—this *very* day—in 1942. In the Battle of the Coral Sea.'

'Oh.' She sounded suitably shocked.

'Weird coincidence, isn't it?' He swallowed the constriction in his throat. Then he smiled at Meg. 'But maybe an even better coincidence is that I am seeing you this evening after all,' he murmured huskily. 'You never know, maybe we're destined for each other, Meg.'

Meg was sure Sam was teasing and she felt more than a little miffed that he might be making fun of her. Lifting her chin defiantly high, she shifted her concentration from his strong, handsome face to their surroundings— the little bay and the moon and the rocky headlands.

Time to leave, or to come up with a quick change of subject. Reluctant to hurry back to her lonely cottage, she changed the subject. 'For some reason, those rocks always remind me of shelled Brazil nuts.'

Sam's eyebrows rose. 'That's an interesting association of ideas. I wonder where it comes from?'

She smiled. 'I know exactly where it comes from. I'm crazy about Brazil nuts.' And for a moment she was absorbed by memory. She was sitting once more at a dining table, laden with Christmas fare, and she could see her father's strong hands wielding the silver nutcracker, breaking open the hard shell and handing her a pure smooth Brazil nut.

'My father always used to crack them for me and, when he gave me one, he would joke… ''Would you like a nut, Meg?'' Of course, his nickname for me was Nutmeg.'

'Nutmeg,' Sam repeated. 'I like that.' He turned to look at her. 'Does your father live here on the island?'

'My father's dead,' she told him in a shaky whisper.

'I'm sorry.' His hand reached out and rubbed her shoulder gently.

'You know he used to warn me that there are no guarantees in life. He reckoned the only thing you can be sure of is that the angles of a triangle will always add up to one hundred and eighty degrees.'

'Sounds like he got one or two nasty shocks along the way.'

'Well, yes. He worked as a draftsman for the same company for thirty-five years and then suddenly they made him redundant.' She snapped her fingers. 'Just like that. Downsizing they called it. Profits were more important than loyal and talented employees.'

Sam's jaw clenched and he swung away so that he no longer looked at her. 'Sometimes the guys running big companies have to make difficult choices.'

'And their answers are always about money,' she responded bitterly.

'Money,' he repeated grimly. His hand was still resting on her and suddenly he smiled at her again and obviously decided to have his own stab at changing the subject. 'As you accepted my apology so nicely this afternoon, we can start afresh, can't we?'

Meg was sure she should have clarified exactly what Sam thought they were *starting*. But perhaps it was the setting, or her loneliness, or even moonlight madness, but she suddenly didn't want to be wary or cautious any more. 'Yes,' she said simply. 'I guess we can.'

'You know,' Sam told her. 'We actually have more in

common than you might be prepared to admit. I used to haunt the Seattle Aquarium when I was a boy. Tell me some more about the reef.'

Realising that he'd cleverly selected a topic she loved to talk about, she was happy to cooperate. 'Something I find very interesting is the coral-spawning that takes place every year. Have you heard about it?'

'I do remember reading something.'

'Marine scientists made the discovery here on this island. Every piece of coral on the Great Barrier Reef, even pieces in buckets and aquariums, becomes fertile and spawns in mass at a certain full moon in spring.' Her eyes danced. 'It's been described as the world's biggest sexual encounter.'

'World's biggest sexual encounter?' Sam repeated with a lazy smile and his gaze speared hers so intently she felt breathless and more than a little warm. 'That's exceptionally interesting.'

She couldn't help chuckling. 'Well, I don't know who actually judges these things.'

He turned towards her so that both his hands could grasp her shoulders. 'I warned you earlier, Meg, I can't resist a challenge.'

His face was in shadow but, as she heard the unmistakable rumble of desire in his voice, flames of unexpected heat darted through Meg. She wondered what she could do about her growing interest in getting close to this man. 'Surely you're not suggesting you want to compete with the entire Great Barrier Reef?' she asked in a strained, tight voice.

'I'm going to make a start.' His gaze centred on her mouth. 'I'm not planning to be upstaged by coral polyps.'

She knew then what was going to happen and she let it.

For the second time, Meg offered absolutely no resistance when he drew her closer. She had a desperate feeling that she had as much chance of resisting Sam Kirby as the tides had of resisting the pull of the moon. Fleetingly, she wondered if this was what destiny felt like.

In spite of her rules about guests, she had never felt so willing, so wanting to be enclosed in a man's arms.

Her heart jolted unsteadily as Sam's lips roamed her mouth and her own lips parted, as open and needy as a desert flower welcoming rain. His kiss deepened and, with a whimper of pleasure, she surrendered to his invasion. Sam tasted wonderful. His hard, strong body felt divine. Wanting more, she crushed herself shamelessly against him, as if she was afraid the world might end any minute and she would miss out on this vital experience.

Yesterday, Sam's kiss had been friendly and gentle. Tonight it quickly became wicked, wild and threatening. And Meg loved it! She loved the heat of his tongue as it plundered her mouth. Loved the hard, intimate force of his body driving and moulding against her.

She heard his desperately ragged breathing and suspected she was rushing headlong into danger. But it was a dark and alluring danger. A danger she suddenly longed for and welcomed.

Flash!

The blinding light startled them both, shattering their embrace.

Meg felt Sam swing angrily out of her arms. 'Get lost!' he cried and began to prowl towards someone in the darkness.

Shaking, Meg followed the direction of his gaze and saw what he'd seen—a man skulking behind a casuarina on the edge of the sand and clutching a camera.

'Let's just get out of here,' Meg called, running after him and grabbing his hand.

For a moment, Sam hesitated, but he shook her hand away and continued to stride towards the darkness in the direction the photographer had taken. There was the sound of a car taking off at speed. 'Who was he?' he demanded, turning back to her. 'I have enough trouble at home with the press.'

'Do you really think it was someone from a newspaper?'

'That's my guess.'

Meg cringed as she thought of all her workmates seeing evidence in tomorrow's paper of her lapse. So much for her personal code of ethics regarding tourists! 'I can't believe I let this happen again,' she whispered to herself.

She supposed she should be grateful to the photographer. He'd broken the spell that had been dragging her towards making a foolish mistake. Heaven knew what might have happened if they hadn't been rudely interrupted.

'Are you worried about your golden rule about kissing guests?' Sam's knuckle grazed her cheek. 'For my part, I'm very glad you broke it. I wouldn't object at all if you wanted to break a few more rules.'

Embarrassed, Meg drew back. 'You know I wasn't going to let you do anything but kiss me.'

'But you *did* let me kiss you,' he challenged. 'And I had the distinct impression that you were kissing me back.'

'I just got carried away with—with the atmosphere and the moonlight.'

'Is that what happened?' His voice suggested that he didn't believe her in the slightest.

'That's all,' she said as convincingly as she could manage. 'And I must go home now.' She had to get out of there before the moonlight or whatever it was started making her reckless again. Turning to head back to her car, she asked, 'Do you need a lift?'

'No. Don't worry about me.' Sam shoved his hands into his pockets and he turned to stare back out to sea.

When she reached her car, Meg looked back at him, but he hadn't moved. And that was good. Maybe it was sinking into Sam's thick skull that they must never take the risk of kissing a third time.

When Sam opened his door the next morning and found Meg standing there, he was mildly surprised. She was wearing a soft, floaty kind of dress that dipped in a low curve from shoulder to shoulder. In her hand was a folded newspaper.

'Good morning,' she greeted him primly, without smiling.

He returned her greeting carefully. 'Morning.'

There was no beating around the bush. Looking somewhere around the centre of his chest, she said, 'Have you seen this morning's paper?'

'Fred phoned and told me about it.'

With an impatient shake of her head, she thrust the paper at him. 'The publicity shot of us with the bottle on the front page is OK, I guess. But take a look at page three. The close-up shot of you and me—'

'On the beach?' Sam supplied as he took the paper and flicked to page three. He looked at the photo and felt his throat tighten. 'That's—er—some clinch, isn't it?'

Meg was blushing. 'What are we going to do about it? Fred wants to make more publicity mileage out of it. He wants us to go to a big function tonight for the handover of the letter—as a couple.'

'Yeah. He explained that when he rang.'

'Don't tell me you agreed?' she asked sharply.

'Sure. Why not?' Sam hoped Meg didn't quiz him too hard about why he'd agreed. He wasn't too sure himself that his motives would stand up to close scrutiny. 'But I take it you're not happy?'

'Of course not!' Meg exclaimed with a haughty lift of her chin that made her look especially stubborn. And gorgeous.

He looked again at the photo. Seeing that image of Meg's arms wrapped around him and her mouth meshed with his was interfering with his search for a rational argument. He tapped the page with a finger and replied in his most nonchalant manner, 'There's not much point in trying to pretend there's nothing between us. Why don't we attend this event together and brazen it out just for this one night?'

Meg stared at him. She looked ready to argue. Her arms were crossed belligerently across her chest and her eyes glistened as she tapped a tattoo with her foot.

Sam waited patiently in silence, unwilling to take the lid off this particular volcano.

Eventually she sighed. 'I'll go to this function on one condition.'

'Yes?'

'We only have the minimum contact necessary to keep the press happy.'

He had been leaning against the door frame, trying to look more casual than he felt. This situation was becoming more ridiculous by the minute, but sharing that opinion with Meg wasn't going to help matters.

Stepping back, he gestured towards the small sitting area in his resort bungalow. 'Why don't you come in? I find this a little difficult to discuss on a doorstep.'

She followed him in silence and assumed a stiff-backed, prudish pose at one end of his couch. Under other circumstances, he might have found it comic.

Selecting a single cane chair, Sam lounged back into the deep cushions. In a deliberately casual movement, he stretched his long legs in front of him, crossing them at the ankles. 'Now, tell me about these conditions of yours.'

She sat straight with her knees together, just as she might have been taught at deportment school, and made a little throat clearing sound. 'What I mean is, there'll be no flirting—no unnecessary touching. We'll just *pretend* we're—a couple who are—um—interested in romance.'

'And of course you're still insisting that you're not the slightest bit interested?'

'I'm certainly not.'

He watched a fascinating pink blush suffuse Meg's cheeks and he tried to ignore his body's inappropriate reaction.

'Just so I'm clear about this; that very romantic kiss on the beach last night—were you pretending, then?'

Her eyes shone with a threatening gleam. 'I told you last night, we can blame the moonlight and the mood for that. It was a slip.'

Remembering the sweet fire of her kiss and just how passionately Meg had *slipped* into his arms, Sam only just managed to keep his face solemn. 'So what do you think will keep the press happy? They already have a picture of us kissing.'

'We just have to be seen together. We can talk.'

'And can we look as if we're enjoying ourselves?'

Her eyes met his and she shrugged. The neckline of her dress slipped a little to reveal a tanned and shapely shoulder. 'I suppose we'll have to look reasonably happy.'

'We might have to dance.'

'Yes.'

'But you want me to hide the fact that I'm attracted to you, Meg?' He deliberately stared at her, trapping her gaze with his.

She stared straight back, her eyes the brilliant, clear grey of Cleveland Bay waters at dusk. 'That's right. You mustn't…' Her courage seemed to falter. Her neat white teeth worried her upper lip.

Sam suppressed a wild urge to leap out of his chair and crush those soft lips with his own, to force them apart, to taste again the sweetness of her mouth. Leaning forward, he dropped his linked hands between his knees. 'OK, fill me in. What mustn't I do?'

'Don't do anything that will make me—'

He waited.

'Don't you dare try to seduce me.'

Sam almost laughed. Here was Meg, looking like a goddess, driving him mad with her soft gold hair, her sea-grey eyes and her delicate air and she was trying to suggest that seduction was *his* agenda. Something he alone schemed and plotted. Something she had no part in.

He rose to his feet and said softly, 'If that's what you want, I'll do my level best not to seduce you, Meg.'

Meg jumped to her feet, too. 'If we have to kiss for any reason—and I can't imagine that there will be one—the lips stay shut.'

'Got you,' he agreed grimly, noting the continued heightening of colour in her cheeks.

'We can hold hands if necessary.'

'OK.'

'Do I need to continue this list of criteria, or do you get the picture?'

Was she serious? 'I think catch your drift.'

She glossed over his sarcasm. 'It's important that there's no misunderstanding.'

It occurred to Sam that this little conference could be more fun than he thought. 'Actually…' he glanced at his watch '…I've got an hour or two to kill. Why don't we make a really long list of all the things I mustn't do to you?'

Meg frowned. On the whole, she'd been relatively happy with this exchange, but had she missed something here? 'I beg your pardon?'

'Come on,' he urged with a slow smile, 'I'd quite like to discuss these rules in minute detail. It could take a while. For example, you've said we must kiss with our lips tight shut, so that means no—'

'I know jolly well what it means.'

'What about touching?' He stepped closer and uninvited little shivers prickled her skin. '*Where* mustn't I touch you? We really should talk about that.'

Meg felt shaky and weak. Obviously, Sam had no idea how much his kiss last night had affected her, or he wouldn't be teasing her like this. Kissing her had just been another bachelor game for him. Bimbo therapy for a bachelor on the loose.

But she hadn't been able to sleep for thinking about the taste of him. And the way he'd made her feel. If he touched her anywhere at this very moment, there was a good chance she would burst into a shower of sparks like an exploding sky-rocket.

'There's no need to discuss this,' she hissed.

'So it's no holds barred?'

'Very funny, Sam.' She walked away from him—out

of the danger zone. Up close, Sam was bad for her mental and emotional health. From the safer distance of the far side of the room, she explained, 'Fred wants us dressed up for tonight like something out of a soap opera.' She looked around the room—anywhere but at him. 'I guess that's appropriate. I feel like I'm caught up in some outlandish soap script.'

'I couldn't have described the situation better myself. That's *exactly* how I feel.'

'It would be easier if someone could hand us a script. Then our roles would be clear.'

He grinned. 'After I've organised to hire a suit, I'm free. We could spend today writing one.'

'Give it a miss, Sam.' She rolled her eyes. 'I'll see you tonight.'

CHAPTER FOUR

THE ONLY evening dress Meg had brought with her when she'd come to work on the island was a soft swirl of silvery grey chiffon over a silk slip with thin spaghetti straps that extended to lace across her bare back. 'I wish I had something with more back,' she told her reflection as she dressed.

If she had to dance with Sam in this dress, the whole business of touching would become a nightmare. His hands couldn't avoid her bare skin.

At exactly seven p.m., he arrived at her bungalow looking predictably scrumptious in a black dinner suit, white shirt and bow tie.

'Good timing,' she said lightly. 'I've just finished an extra coat of mascara—for the benefit of the photographers, of course.'

Her evening bag and a gauzy wrap lay ready on the dining table and she turned to gather them up. And heard his low whistle.

'That's some dress you're wearing.' His voice was rough as if he'd swallowed beach pebbles.

Half turning back in his direction, she found him looking at her with a puzzled smile. His eyes were paying fascinated attention to her exposed back. And she read admiration and interest in his gaze. This was going to be worse than she expected!

'You're planning to dance with me this evening wearing *this*?' He gestured to the criss-crossing of silvery ribbon that held her dress together. 'And—and you expect me to avoid all those no-go areas on that list of yours?'

'This is all I have that's suitable,' she muttered. 'You'll manage, Sam.'

They stood looking at each other, while the room seemed to vibrate with a thousand things they'd left unsaid.

Sam let out his breath. 'Of course I'll manage. As I've already warned you, I've never been known to knock back a challenge.' He offered his elbow so that she could link her arm through his. 'Allow me to escort you, Ms Bennet.'

Scooping up her bag and wrap, she stepped towards him and rested a cautious hand on the inside of his elbow. Her fingers met the luxurious silk and wool blend of his coat. He murmured close to her ear, 'You look much more beautiful than any soap star.'

Just in time, she remembered not to smile. 'No smooth talk, Prince Charming,' she warned.

'Spoilsport,' he muttered back, and they left her place and made their way through the tropical gardens to the restaurant.

A florid-faced Fred, dressed in an uncomfortably tight dinner suit and an outlandish rainbow-coloured bow tie, looked halfway between a clown and an Italian tenor as he rushed towards them. 'Our VIPs!' he gushed. He planted a noisy wet kiss on Meg's cheek and embraced Sam as if he were a long-lost brother. 'You two look great.' His eyes narrowed. 'Have you got your act together? No bickering?'

'Absolutely,' replied Sam. He draped a possessive arm across Meg's bare shoulders. 'We're totally smitten. Can't keep our hands off each other.'

Meg shot a scowl in his direction, but he wasn't looking. He was too busy smiling at her boss, while his thumb trailed devastating, lazy circles around the nub of her shoulder.

'Fantastic!' Fred beamed. He gestured to the gaily decorated dining room. From every table balloons floated above old bottles encrusted with glued-on sand. Fred was proud of his stroke of decorative genius. The assembled guests, mainly business associates of Fred's as well as the media, were all staring at Sam and Meg with undisguised curiosity.

Fred winked at Sam. 'Everyone's dying to meet you.'

As they progressed across the room, cameras flashed and Sam kept his arm firmly around Meg's shoulders. Through her teeth, she muttered, 'You're getting a bit carried away!'

'Don't panic,' he murmured, dropping his head so that his mouth was low against her ear. Her heart seemed to tremble in her chest when he whispered softly, as a lover might, 'Just remember it's only a game. And it will all be over in an hour or two.'

In an hour or two? Meg feared by then all that would be left of her would be a melted puddle. She reminded herself that Sam had a string of girlfriends at home on the other side of the world and that was exactly why she had to resist his charm. That was what she had to concentrate on.

'Don't pull away from me,' he ordered under his breath, as they reached a circle of guests. He dropped an unexpected kiss on her cheek. 'That's better. Just relax and enjoy.'

Relax and enjoy? No way. She had been relaxed when she'd first met Sam Kirby. Red Riding Hood had been relaxed when she'd met the wolf. She and Red Riding

Hood had both been very foolish young women. Tonight she planned to keep her alarm systems on high alert.

But it was intensely annoying that Sam could play his part so easily.

While dizzying, wild sensations danced along her skin, he remained cool and detached. He charmed Fred's guests by answering their questions and showing polite interest in their businesses and, at the same time, he kept her at constant fever pitch with casual touches and killer smiles.

When a photographer approached from behind, Sam had the audacity to run a daring finger down Meg's exposed spine. And when she reacted sharply, he smiled and whispered, 'Stay cool. This is just to keep Fred happy.'

Several cameras flashed.

A woman asked, 'When you return to the States, will you take Meg with you?'

'Oh, no!' Meg responded quickly.

Sam's hand squeezed her shoulder as he hauled her companionably against him. 'Meg and I have an understanding.'

With some difficulty, Meg muffled a gasp of dismay. Up close against him, his tantalising aftershave was distressingly arousing and she had the greatest difficulty speaking two sensible words in a row. She offered the woman a shaky smile.

'We're going to hate to be apart,' Sam added. His blue eyes twinkled as he smiled at Meg. 'Aren't we, sweetheart?'

'I'll—I'll be counting the days till he comes back,' she managed to reply.

To her relief, a meal was served and there was a chance to remove herself from Sam and sit down. Not that she was hungry. With him still at her side, her stomach was so tied in knots, she doubted her food would stay down.

'Having fun?' he asked and Meg noticed he wasn't having any difficulty wolfing down seafood and salad.

She crumbled a bread roll with nervous fingers. 'Not much.'

'What's the problem?'

'I think you're overdoing it.'

His eyes widened, pleading innocence, while his smile looked as guilty as sin. 'Overdoing what exactly?'

'As if you didn't know.'

'But I've stuck to your rules.'

'You have not,' she answered sharply. 'You're making up your own rules.'

He leaned closer and his thumb caressed her lower lip. 'You look gorgeous, Meg, but you're pouting when you should be smiling. Don't forget, as far as everyone here is concerned, we're at the beginning of a thrilling new romance. You're mad about me, baby.'

'As far as I'm concerned, I'm mad *at* you, not about you.'

'It's showing.' He touched her frowning forehead. 'The problem is,' he said, in a roughened whisper, 'I *want* to touch you and hold you and kiss you. It's not an effort for me at all.'

Meg dropped her gaze to her plate. Angrily she stabbed her fork into a pile of shredded lettuce. There could only be one reason why Sam found this ordeal so effortless.

He wasn't affected the way she was. She was burning up with every glance and touch, while he remained completely in control. This whole evening was just an amusing game for him. He was a love-'em-and-leave-'em millionaire, who was used to getting anything he wanted.

'If you've had enough to eat, I'd love to dance with you, Meg.'

She sighed. The band was playing a popular number and couples were leaving the tables for the dance floor. 'Do we have to?'

His gaze took in her dress. 'That's a dress designed for dancing.' Standing, he held out his hand. 'I promise this will be painless.'

I very much doubt that, Sam. Slowly, she rose to her feet.

His warm hand rested on her bare lower back as he steered her towards the dance floor. In a daze, she allowed him to take her hand in his, while she placed the other on his shoulder. She felt the hush of his breath against her hair. Slowly, without touching, their bodies swayed to the music. Then Sam began to move, leading her confidently. She sensed the strength and athletic grace of his body as he moved.

'Now, this isn't too difficult, is it?' he teased.

'No,' she whispered, feeling a surge of anger that gave her a new lease of strength.

It suddenly occurred to her that this man was far too self-assured and smug for his own good. And if he could dredge up this kind of will-power then, by Jove, so could she. It was time to listen to her head instead of her hormones.

It was payback time. Time to discover if Sam could handle the kind of treatment he'd been dishing out. Meg snuggled in a little closer.

Immediately she sensed his surprise.

'I'm going to play this your way,' she whispered huskily. 'After all, we only have this one night together, don't we?'

'Uh-huh.' He grunted his reply.

Resting her head against his shoulder, she did her best to ignore how good it felt to nestle against his strength. 'Is this what you want?' she asked.

Sam cleared his throat. 'Sure.'

'I admit I was being childish about all those rules,' she murmured. When he didn't reply, she slipped her hand out of his and wound both arms around his neck. By holding her breath, she was just able to keep the most sizzling zones of her body a hair's breadth from his. 'I must admit you have marvellous self-control.'

'Meg,' Sam asked, 'have you been drinking?'

'I've had half a glass of wine. Why?'

'You're acting—different.'

'Am I?' She raised innocent eyes to his.

She realised it was a mistake as soon as she saw the heat flaring in Sam's blue gaze.

'You know you're playing with fire.' He growled the words and his hands cradled her hips and he hauled her closer. '*This* is how much control I have.'

In a microsecond, her sensitive breasts were moulded against his hard chest...his thigh slid audaciously between hers...and dramatic evidence of his lack of control thrust against her.

Shocked, Meg quivered. Hot shafts of equally out of control feelings raced through her. Before she could protest or gather her wits, Sam held her even closer and his lips lowered over hers.

'Sam.' She spluttered his name.

'Keep your lips shut,' he murmured against her mouth, 'or you're in deep, deep trouble.'

But Meg knew she was already in all kinds of trouble. Leg-trembling, brain-melting trouble. The restaurant's lights had been lowered and, to the background crooning of a sultry saxophone, Sam held her close and danced slowly—very, very slowly.

Hardly conscious of her own movement, her senses were completely focused on the shocking yet wonderful way his body surged against hers and the way his mouth moved over her with admirable attention to detail.

And she was matching each wicked move of his with one of her own.

Vaguely, she realised that her plan to unsettle Sam was backfiring, but she was rapidly reaching a stage beyond caring. Her body was becoming fused with his in a slow meltdown that made common sense and the rest of the world fade away.

She didn't notice the music had stopped until a rude tap-tap-tapping on the microphone startled her out of her trance.

'Can I have your attention, ladies and gentlemen?'

As they looked up, Fred smirked in their direction.

Meg stepped away from Sam. Feeling suddenly cold and foolish, she stood stiffly self-conscious among the dancers still on the floor.

In the spotlight, Fred took a gulp from a wineglass and looked self-important. 'You all know why we're gathered here this evening. I've always been a sentimental sort of a bloke, and I wanted my friends to join me to celebrate this special occasion. Around sixty years ago, an American called Tom Kirby was facing the possibility of death in the middle of the Coral Sea and he sent a message—a love letter—to his wife. Two weeks ago, our very own Meg Bennet found that message.'

He paused for a polite burst of applause.

'And Tom's grandson, Sam, has come here to claim this letter. It contains some very important information for his family. Now…' Fred beamed, picking up the bottle and the letter from the table beside him '...if Sam could just come up here...' He looked around. 'Are the photographers ready?'

Meg watched as Sam, with shoulders squared and dark head arrogantly high, made his way to the microphone. She stood, three fingers pressed against the lips he'd so recently been kissing, as he shook Fred's hand, received the bottle and letter, and turned to the microphone. Fred adjusted it slightly to accommodate Sam's extra height.

When she'd first met him, she'd thought he looked like a film star. Tonight, he looked like a conquering hero as he waved the bottle triumphantly above his head and everyone cheered and clapped. 'This is a very special moment,' he began by saying. 'Wars do terrible things to families and this war robbed my father of the chance to know his dad, Tom Kirby.'

He paused and seemed to take a deep breath as he held the bottle out in front of him. 'Soon, I'll be able to place this bottle in my father's hands. Dad will be able to read for himself the letter Tom wrote to my grandmother.'

Meg's heart swelled with emotion and tears filled her eyes. It was happening again. Every time she thought about the bottle and the time it had spent at sea, she became totally caught up in the magic mystery of it.

'Of course none of this could have happened without one incredibly important person,' Sam continued. 'The woman who found the bottle—Meg Bennet.'

The spotlight from the stage suddenly caught her in its glare. Sam was standing with his arm outstretched towards her. Everyone was looking at her. People were clapping. Sam was smiling his sexiest, most heart-wrenching smile. Prince Charming.

She couldn't smile back, she was too busy holding back tears.

He looked down at the letter in his hand. The room was quiet, waiting for him to wrap up his speech.

The spotlight drew back and Meg had never been so grateful for shadows. Her heart was beating so loudly, its drumming filled her ears. Sam was saying something else, but she couldn't hear him. She was thinking of how she'd felt just now as she'd danced with him.

Tonight, it seemed so fitting that the bottle had brought this beautiful man from across the sea. To her. She had a very strong feeling that she was as helpless as a rock plunging off a precipice. Despite her best efforts to resist, she was falling in love.

Sam finished speaking. There was loud applause. He smiled some more, but, glad to get out of the limelight, he excused himself as soon as possible and made his way through the crowd towards Meg.

He grinned and shook the letter at her. 'Got it at last.' Then he looked at her more closely and frowned. 'You look upset. What's wrong?'

'Nothing.' She replied so faintly he probably couldn't hear her. After all the fuss she'd made this morning about rules, how could she tell him she'd changed her mind? She suddenly wanted him to go on kissing and holding her for the rest of the century.

He gave an embarrassed little shrug. 'I got a bit carried away before on the dance floor.'

Her gaze dropped to her hands, but she couldn't stop her lips from twitching into a smile. 'You were very badly behaved.'

'You want to get out of here?'

'Yes,' she muttered quickly. 'I'll just get my things.'

Together they made the necessary farewells and then walked back to Meg's bungalow along lamp-lit paths that wound through tropical shrubbery.

When they reached her door, she opened it and stepped inside. Sam followed quickly as if he expected her to try to lock him out.

She didn't have a clue what would happen now. And she wasn't sure what she wanted to happen. Her mind was at war with her heart and her wayward body. In her head, she knew she should be politely showing Sam straight back out the front door. But her body was urging him to stay close. Really close.

And her heart kept whispering to her about destiny.

'Do you want to read the letter?' she asked him.

'Yeah. I'll take a quick look at it.'

Meg kept her distance, allowing Sam to read in complete privacy.

She knew half of it off by heart anyhow. The part she loved was where Tom had written, *'Sweetheart, I want you to know that meeting you, knowing you, loving you is the most wonderful thing that ever happened to me. You've given my life shape and splendour.'*

'It's beautiful, isn't it?' she asked when Sam looked up.

He nodded his head slowly, his eyes returning to the piece of fragile paper.

'Do you want to ring your lawyers or your family?'

'Later.' He placed it and the bottle carefully on her dining table and stood stiffly in the middle of her small living room, looking distractingly handsome in his dark evening suit. 'Right now I want to figure out what's going on in your head.'

'About the letter?' she asked, confused.

'No. About us. About rules and conditions.'

'I'm giving myself a strict lecture,' she said quickly.

'So you should,' he replied with mock severity. 'All

those rules you've broken.' His face broke into a cheeky, boyish smile. 'But you know what they say about rules.'

Warning bells pealed in her head. But, she couldn't listen. Not any more. She couldn't bear it if Sam walked away now. She had to ignore them. 'I've heard that they are made to be broken.'

'Yeah,' he whispered. 'And that's what we're going to do now, Meg.' His smoky gaze roamed over her. 'We're going to break all your rules. One by one. Come here.'

Unable to resist, she walked towards him, her eyes fixed on his, until she was within arm's reach. Then she stopped.

'I think the first rule was about holding hands,' he murmured.

'We were allowed to hold hands.'

He held up his hands in front of him and, as her heart thumped, Meg placed her own against his, palm to palm. For heated seconds they stood, facing each other and her legs trembled. Slowly Sam slid his long fingers between each of hers till they were clasped, then he pulled her close till their lips touched and, against her mouth, he whispered, 'Next we need to break your kissing rule.'

His tongue traced a seductive line between her lips and they drifted open. And then his lips and tongue began to explore her mouth at a teasing, leisurely pace, and Meg wondered how such an easy, slow touch could ignite such a wild and violent longing. She was helpless to prevent herself from melting against him.

Dazed, with a drowsy, heated hunger, she threw her arms around Sam's neck and dragged him closer. She clung to him, craving more. 'Please, forget about rules.'

The shudder she felt in his strong frame and the responding clamour of her own body shocked her. An instant later, his kiss became urgent, deep and intensely intimate. The same shocking heat and wildness that she'd felt on the dance floor surged through Meg again.

She wasn't sure what excited her more—her own wild sensations or Sam's obvious delight in her. He began a lingering discovery of her bare back, playing with the lacing as he went.

Her breathing grew more and more ragged as his hands trailed slowly up to her shoulders. Tucking his thumbs under the tiny straps, he slipped them from her shoulders, before he settled his hands lower, cupping her breasts.

Meg shivered with delectable suspense and he whispered, 'You're so beautiful—just beautiful.'

Her body hummed with exquisite anticipation…while her fevered imagination raced ahead. And she could see the next few moments unfurling…herself and Sam shedding their clothes…until skin touched to skin.

She sizzled at the thought.

Except.

Except…*other* thoughts crept into her mind…*annoying, sensible thoughts.*

This man was famous in Seattle as a love-'em-and-leave-'em bachelor. Could she, *should* she trust him with her body?

Another fleeting misgiving flashed into Meg's mind. Her father had been too reserved to discuss romance, but she suspected that if her mother had lived to talk of such things she would have warned Meg about the folly of falling in love and making love all on the same evening.

Sam must have sensed her hesitation. He pulled back a little. 'You OK?' he whispered against her cheek.

Suddenly nervous, she whispered. 'I—I don't know.'

His hands stilled and, for a moment, he simply held her gently. 'I can't believe how I feel about you,' he murmured softly, close to her ear.

'What way would that be?' she had to ask, her heart thumping wildly.

Gently he settled her shoulder straps back in place and, cradling her face with his hands, he looked deep into her eyes. 'Like…like I've found something I didn't know I was searching for. But—'

Meg pressed her fingers to his lips. 'Don't say any more,' she breathed. 'That's scary.'

He leaned back a little, studying her face carefully. 'Scary nice or scary scary?'

'Scary amazing,' she whispered. 'It's exactly how I feel about you.'

He let out a rush of breath and gathered her close again. 'Oh, Nutmeg,' he said softly, a husky tremor in his voice. 'You don't mind if I call you Nutmeg?'

'No.'

'It's a name that sounds just right for a woman who has a touch of spice that makes her incredibly delicious.'

Her lips wavered into a shaky smile.

For a minute they stood close, their hearts pounding against each other's chest.

'This is going to happen, Meg. We both know that. But there's no need to rush. Am I rushing you?'

Meg couldn't answer. She was shaking and she had no idea what to say.

But a sudden vision of the distant future seized her! Maybe one day, when she was a little old lady, she would think about finding the bottle and she would remember Sam Kirby and she would wonder…

Sam's fingers were gently massaging the nape of her neck. She looked up into his face and saw his obvious desire warring with such a tender concern for her that her heart sang. He cared. Why had she ever doubted? She loved this man.

'Sam, you're not rushing me,' she told him.

'You're sure?' His voice sounded raspy.

The next moment, his strong arms began to enfold her once more and she knew with a beautiful certainty that this was the one place in the world she wanted to be. Sam made her feel vibrantly thrillingly alive.

She nodded against his chest. 'I'm sure,' she whispered.

Without a moment's hesitation, he lowered his head once more and again his lips began to work their heated magic, travelling on a sensual, mind-numbing journey, exploring her neck and then her ear and finally her mouth.

All doubts vaporised.

'I want you to stay,' she whispered.

CHAPTER FIVE

SAM woke first, just as the sun broke through the overhead trees and sent dappled light through the filmy curtains. Beside him, Meg lay with her hair tumbling over her face and one arm curled to hug her pillow. His heart swelled as he thought of the night they'd shared.

Carefully, he brushed her hair, soft as corn silk, away from her face so he could see the delicate outline of her profile against the snowy pillow. The urge to kiss her awake, to take her in his arms and make love to her again was overpowering.

But he resisted the impulse. Who knew where the media mafia were hanging out, or what sordid story they would concoct? To be fair to Meg, he should leave now—quickly and discreetly—before the resort workers were up and about.

He eased himself off the bed and dressed without making a sound. In bare feet, he padded out into her small living area. He looked around curiously, hungry for details that would tell him more about Meg.

Usually he was careful to retain a healthy ignorance about the domestic details of his women friends. As a confirmed bachelor, he'd found it safer that way. Women had an annoying habit of quickly jumping to the wrong conclusions if a guy showed interest in their day-to-day lives.

But Meg made him feel both incredibly curious and dangerously reckless. Right now, he didn't care what conclusions she came to. They were probably on the right track.

Not that this simple, tidy cabin, combining a neat little kitchen with a dining and sitting area, gave too many clues about Meg. The bowl of fruit on the kitchen counter held the usual healthy varieties. A cluster of spice bottles stood beside the stove.

Everything seemed very orderly, but the cottage had a temporary feel about it, as if Meg had brought few of her personal possessions with her. The only thing remotely out of place was a half-completed jigsaw puzzle on the coffee table.

He smiled. Meg probably collected a library of books, games and puzzles to keep less active guests entertained. This puzzle was of a painting by the ancient Italian master, Botticelli. It was called *La Primavera*. Spring.

Sam's smile lingered. The beautiful woman in the puzzle was dressed in a soft gauzy gown covered in flowers. She had a face like Meg's, sweet and slightly serious. Her hair was long and fair and her beautiful eyes were an indeterminate colour that might have been green, or grey or...blue? She reminded him so much of Meg that he almost headed back to the bedroom.

He spotted the piece of puzzle that depicted the spring maiden's bare pink foot and, picking it up, he fitted it into place.

Then he released his breath on a weary, drawn out sigh. If only his life could be as simple as that. Could it really be just a matter of finding the puzzle pieces and slotting them together? He'd tried to reassure himself that when this letter was handed over, everything would fall into place neatly. Kirby & Son's holdings would be safe and he could start planning a future.

He wanted to give a good deal of thought to his future.

Sitting on Meg's rattan sofa, he pulled on his socks and shoes, then quietly let himself out by the back door and made his way, as unobtrusively as possible, back to his own bungalow.

He'd showered and changed, and eaten breakfast from a tray delivered to his door when the phone rang. Draining the last of his coffee, he snatched up the receiver. 'Sam Kirby.'

'Good morning, Sam.'

The sound of Meg's voice unleashed a hot yearning, catching him unawares. He took a deep breath. 'How are you this morning, Nutmeg?'

'Fine—wonderful.' she purred the words. 'And you?'

'Missing you.'

'Yes,' she said softly. 'I miss you, too.'

'I didn't want to stir up trouble by hanging around at your place this morning.'

'I realised that. Thanks. Have you seen this morning's paper?'

Sam groaned and dragged stiff fingers through his hair as he thought of the possibilities. 'Not yet. I take it you have?'

'Yes. It's not as bad as I thought it might be, although now they're tagging this story as "Love in a bottle".'

'Sounds like an ad for alcohol or something.'

'There's another photo of us at the party in an embarrassing clinch.' After a pause she added, 'I hope you don't mind, Sam.'

Hearing the tension vibrating in her voice, Sam frowned. 'How do you feel about it?'

'I'm not too bothered.'

'You sound bothered.'

'That's—that's because of something else that's come

up. A couple of minutes ago I had a phone call from a little old lady.'

He felt instantly defensive. His hand gripped the phone more tightly. 'Don't tell me someone is giving you a lecture about your wicked ways?'

'No, Sam, it's probably worse than that.'

'How?' he snapped.

'She's claiming that she's Tom Kirby's wife and that the letter in the bottle is for her.'

Oh, God! Sam's heart thudded. He slumped against the wall beside him. 'Who the hell is this person?'

'Her name is Dolly Kirby. She lives on the mainland and she says she met and married Tom when he was based in this district during the war.'

Sweat was breaking out all over Sam. Dolly *Kirby?* Under his breath, he cursed and he rubbed the back of his hand over his damp forehead. 'I don't believe it.' He groaned. 'It can't be true. It can't be. Tom Kirby was already married to my grandmother before he left for the war. My grandmother was already pregnant with my father.'

'I agree this is really weird,' Meg admitted. 'Dolly doesn't want to talk to the papers,' she added gently, as if to calm him. 'She wanted to talk to me first. To us, actually.'

Sam closed his eyes and tried to think clearly, rationally. The fact that this woman didn't want to run to the press with her story had to be a good thing, didn't it? But hell! What on earth was going on here?

Meg spoke again. 'She sounds very sweet.'

'Does she, now?' he replied slowly as, out of nowhere, a pack of nasty suspicions raised their ugly, yapping heads. Just when he thought he had this business safely in hand, a new problem emerged. 'It sounds fishy to me.'

'*Sam?*' Meg's tone sharpened. He could hear the note of reproach in that one syllable. 'You should at least meet Dolly before you start jumping to conclusions.'

'Yeah.' He sighed. 'I'll meet her.'

'Fred's given me instructions to be at your—um—disposal today. We could go across to Townsville later this morning. There are quite a few ferry times to choose from.'

'OK.' Sam pinched the bridge of his nose between a finger and thumb. 'And, Meg...'

'Yes?'

'Let me handle this. We need to approach this whole exercise with extreme caution.'

'For heaven's sake, Sam. I think you're overreacting. We're going to check out a little old lady, not a hideaway for armed terrorists.'

He heard the iciness chilling her voice and, not for the first time, Sam wished he could forget the family business. Throw off his responsibilities to Kirby & Son. Surely, when a guy met a woman like Meg, he should be able to put the rest of his life on hold? He would give anything to forget about the will and to take Meg in his arms again.

And keep her there.

As they stood at Dolly Kirby's front gate, Meg and Sam exchanged wary smiles. During the ferry ride across from the island, Sam had been withdrawn and subdued and Meg had tried hard not to let her disappointment show.

She'd been following her instincts when she'd asked Sam to stay last night and those instincts had led her to the most sensational, magical evening of her entire life.

Today the bubble had burst.

It seemed that Sam was in danger of losing his millions

and it was clear where his priorities lay. The attentive lover, the fascinated, delighted companion of yesterday had been replaced by a cool, serious stranger.

Seeing him like this left a chilling, sad emptiness like a cold hollow around Meg's heart. Now she realised she'd been jumping the gun to imagine that last night's happiness had been based on a blossoming of reciprocal love—the kind of love that lasts.

She would give anything for just one of yesterday's smiles.

He reached forward and opened the latch on the rusty metal gate. It squeaked on its hinges as he shoved it open and he gestured for Meg to go before him. When they reached the low set of wooden steps leading to the front veranda of the cottage, his hand rested lightly at the small of her back. She noted with a grim smile that, even when he was dreadfully worried, his natural courtesy remained intact.

Dolly Kirby answered Sam's knock almost immediately.

'Oh, my goodness!' Her pale blue eyes riveted on Sam. They were rounded with shock. 'Oh, my dear Lord!'

Meg thought for a moment that the old lady was going to faint.

Sam dipped his head stiffly. 'Good morning, ma'am.'

Dolly continued to stare at him while her mouth trembled and her arthritic fingers clutched at the big brass doorknob as if for support.

'Mrs—er—Kirby?' Sam asked in clarification.

She nodded and at last she spoke. 'Yes. I'm sorry but you gave me such a shock. You—you look so much like him.'

'Him?'

Meg glanced at Sam and watched his face darken with discomfort.

'My Tom. His eyes were that beautiful sky blue just like yours—and with your dark hair. Oh, dear, you look so much like my Tom, and you sound just like him, too.'

Dolly's eyes glistened with sudden tears. Meg felt her own throat grow prickly with emotion. 'Dolly, I'm Meg Bennet. You spoke to me on the phone and, as you've guessed, this is Sam Kirby.'

Tentative handshakes were exchanged.

'Please, come inside.' Dolly led the way down the central hallway of her simple home and then turned into her lounge. She stood in the middle of the room and indicated they should sit on the old-fashioned, overstuffed sofa. When Meg and Sam were seated and leaning back against the frilly hand-embroidered cushions, she took her place on a carved wooden chair and continued to stare at Sam. 'I can't get over the likeness,' she whispered. 'It's like Tom walked back into my life.'

He cleared his throat. 'So—er—Dolly, you're claiming to have married my grandfather.'

'Yes, dear.' She nodded her head vehemently. 'Tom and I were married in April, 1942. Just before he headed off for the Battle of the Coral Sea.'

Meg wished Sam didn't look quite so stony, like a lawyer grilling a suspect in the witness box.

'There can't have been much time for a long courtship?'

'No, there wasn't. I think I shocked my family.' Dolly's face trembled into a wistful smile. 'It was a whirlwind romance.'

Meg felt a rush of understanding, of having shared the experience of falling in love with a Kirby at breakneck speed. She couldn't help smiling back at Dolly. If Tom

Kirby had looked even half as sexy as Sam—if he had smiled at Dolly with the same heart-stopping blue eyes as Sam's—she had no doubt at all that the other woman had fallen in love with the pace of a lightning strike.

She sensed Sam sitting even more stiffly beside her.

'You have evidence? A marriage licence?' he asked in the deceptively casual tone of a policeman making routine inquiries.

Meg bit her lip uneasily. She wished he could take the trouble to be more gentle with this elderly woman.

But, despite her fragile frame, Dolly was sprightly for her age. She was on her feet in a moment and crossing the carpeted room to an old-fashioned, beautifully carved sideboard. She picked up a framed photograph and a tattered manila folder and brought them across to him.

The black and white photograph in its delicate silver frame shook in her frail hand as she offered it. 'That's Tom and I. It was taken just before we were married.'

As Meg leaned closer to look at the picture he held, she bumped against Sam's shoulder and she tried not to think about how much she loved the feel of him against her. She focused on the details of the photograph and tiny, sensitive hairs rose on the back of her neck.

The laughing young man in the photo could have been Sam.

His height and build were very similar, but it was in their faces that the two men bore such a startling resemblance: the bright eyes, despite the lack of colour in the photo, the thick black hair; the strong line of the dark brows; the slightly crooked nose and squared, no-nonsense jaw. And the mouth; Meg could see that even Tom Kirby's lips were exactly like Sam's—surprisingly sensuous in such a strongly masculine face.

Her eyes caught Dolly's and they exchanged shy

smiles as a flash of sympathetic understanding sparked between them.

Behind the couple rose a familiar rocky headland.

'That looks like Florence Bay,' Meg cried out.

'Yes, dear.' Dolly smiled wistfully. 'Tom and I met on the island. Florence was a very special place for us.'

'You know, that's where I found the bottle?'

Dolly nodded and her face shone.

Sam made throat-clearing noises and shifted uneasily.

Meg looked at the young Dolly in the photo with her hand resting possessively on Tom Kirby's arm, demonstrating the same sense of connection and belonging that she felt for Sam.

The parallels were so strong, Meg couldn't help remembering the strange, mystical bond she'd felt when she'd found the bottle. It was as if she'd been caught up in some kind of time warp.

Dolly spoke. 'I had never been one to chase after boys. I didn't really know much about—er—passion. But with Tom, it was love at first sight and it was a love so big that neither of us could hold back.'

Meg was quite certain she understood. People *could* fall in love in a heartbeat. Look what had happened to her last night.

She thought with a sigh, poor Dolly. She'd met Tom, had loved him and had lost him in such a short space of time. She couldn't bear the thought of losing Sam when she'd only just begun to know him.

'Well, there...' Sam began to speak, but his voice cracked and he had to start again. 'There is certainly a strong family likeness.'

Dolly nodded. 'It's quite remarkable, isn't it?' She opened the manila folder. 'And here's the wedding certificate.'

In silence, Sam accepted the folder. Meg sat back and watched his face as he read the details carefully. She wished there was something she could do to make this easier for him. He looked so grim and worried. She would have loved to stroke that furrowed brow, or to kiss away the tension in those unsmiling lips.

Dolly spoke softly. 'I'm afraid we had to get married very quietly in a civil ceremony. The navy wouldn't have given Tom permission to marry in the middle of active duty, so it was all rather clandestine.'

Sam's expression grew darker than ever. He handed the photo and folder back to Dolly. 'Thank you for showing me these.'

After Dolly put them on a small side table, she sat down again opposite them.

Sam cleared his throat and nodded towards the folder on the table. 'I might have to let my lawyers take a look at that licence at some stage.'

Dolly nodded. 'I don't mind.' Her eyes gleamed as she smiled at him 'I would love to read Tom's letter.'

'Oh, Dolly, I hope you can see it soon.' Meg couldn't hold back her emotional outburst. 'It's just the most beautiful message.'

Sam swung around and glared at her. 'We still have to determine who it was written for,' he said coldly.

'Ease off, Sam,' Meg murmured reproachfully. *How could he be so hard? Couldn't he tell how disturbing all this must be for Dolly?*

His eyes met hers, read her dismay and flicked away again. He addressed the old lady. 'You know that my grandfather was already married before he left the States?'

For a long, awkward moment, Dolly stared at him,

open-mouthed. Slowly she began to shake her head. 'Oh, no, dear. I'm quite certain he wasn't.'

Sam's voice rose. 'Of course he was. My grandmother was already expecting a baby—my father.'

Dolly's gaze lowered and she fiddled nervously with the pleated skirt of her blue floral dress. Her lower lip trembled. 'I don't know anything about a baby. When I read in the paper that Tom had a grandson, I was quite shocked.'

'There was most definitely a baby. My father's name was Jefferson Thomas Kirby. He was born in 1942.'

'I'm sure Tom didn't know anything about a baby either.' After a pause, Dolly added, 'That's sad.' She raised her glistening eyes again and bit her lip. 'Tom told me about his fiancée. Her name was Judith, wasn't it?'

A strangling sound emitted from Sam's throat. Meg watched with alarm as a red tinge crept along his cheekbones and reached the tips of his ears. He drew in a sharp breath. 'Judith was my grandmother's name.'

Straightening her elderly shoulders as much as she could, Dolly spoke slowly, directing her gaze steadily at Sam. 'I am quite certain Tom and Judith were never married. He told me he would contact Judith and break off the engagement just as soon as he could. I know he tried, but I never heard if she received the message.'

Meg felt Sam's shock reverberate through his body. He slumped as if he'd been slugged with something heavy.

'You didn't try to contact her at all...after...afterwards?' he asked.

'Oh, yes.' Dolly sighed. 'I wrote several letters to Tom's family in Seattle during the war—and after the war. None of them was ever answered. If I'd had the money, I would have travelled over there to try to find someone.'

Slipping her hand into Sam's, Meg squeezed gently, but if he noticed he didn't acknowledge her attempt at sympathy. He seemed dazed.

'This is all very strange,' he said at last. Then, as if the fog cleared, he shook his head and snapped to alert attention again. 'I'm going to have to consult with my lawyers before we can—take this any further.'

He stood abruptly, letting Meg's hand slip out of his as if he hadn't even noticed it was there. She struggled to send Dolly a reassuring smile.

'Thanks for—for informing us. Good afternoon,' Sam said with a stiff little nod of his head. Then he frowned at Dolly. 'And I'd prefer if you kept this just between ourselves for the moment.'

'Of course.'

The three of them made their way back down the narrow hall to the front door. There was a hurried, unsatisfactory exchange of farewells, then Sam took off down the path with Meg following. She turned and offered one final little wave to Dolly before getting into the car.

They headed back into the city. Meg drove the car Fred had provided for use on the mainland, while Sam sank back in the passenger's seat and released his breath in a long, drawn-out sigh.

'That was tough,' she suggested as she turned into the main road.

He leaned an elbow on the windscreen ledge and rubbed his forehead slowly. 'This whole business about Dolly just doesn't make any kind of sense.'

'It must be a shock for both of you.'

'I can't believe my grandfather would...'

Sam shook his head as he left the obvious dangling.

He found it so hard to believe that his grandfather had been married to anyone else but Judith Kirby. When he was little, he'd been more than a touch afraid of his grandmother. She was a haughty, snobbish woman—who had always dressed impeccably and found small boys rather noisy and troublesome. She had been highly regarded in Seattle's best social circles.

Later, when he'd grown tall and had developed less noisy habits, she had favoured him more fondly. He wondered now, how she'd felt when he'd grown to look so much like Tom Kirby. He was mildly surprised that she'd never commented on the fact.

How would she have reacted to this news from Dolly? What would she have said to the possibility that her husband had committed bigamy? Of course, she would have dismissed the notion as rubbish.

It had to be rubbish.

The thought of his grandmother refuting such an idea with a toss of her silver hair and a sniff of her patrician nose reassured him for a moment. A very short moment.

But the evidence of that photo and the certificate was a little hard to ignore. If the documents were frauds, they'd been prepared by professionals.

He pressed tense fingers against his forehead. Of course, it wasn't beyond the realms of possibility that one of Kirby & Son's competitors had a hand in all this.

'A penny for your thoughts.' Meg's warm voice penetrated his speculations.

'You wouldn't like them.' He sighed. He had seen the way she'd been so caught up in Dolly's story. If the little old lady was a fraud, Meg would be devastated.

'Cheer up.' Her hand lifted from the gear stick to give his a friendly squeeze.

He sent her an attempt at a smile. Damn it, the last

thing he wanted to be doing with Meg was sifting through the sordid details of his grandfather's love life. They should be adding a few interesting details to their own.

'Sorry you had to get mixed up in this,' he told her.

'I started it,' she reminded him, flashing him a quick grin. 'I was the one who found the bottle. Maybe I should have just left it stuck in the sand.' She steered the car into the car park next to the ferry terminal. Once she had parked, she said. 'A necessary change of subject. Did you want to do anything else before you head back to the island?'

Reaching over, he touched her soft cheek. 'Changing the subject is an excellent idea.'

In the past, when the pressure of work had threatened to overwhelm him, he'd developed a habit of deliberately focusing on something else for an hour or two. He'd always come back to the problem with a clearer head. Often he'd drive off into the mountains of Seattle's hinterland. Sometimes he'd visit his favourite childhood haunt—the Aquarium.

He smiled at Meg. 'If we could shop for some exotic ingredients, would you let me into that neat little kitchen of yours, so I could cook dinner tonight?'

Her eyes widened and he noted that her irises reflected hints of the mint-green colour of her dress. 'You can cook?' she asked, her smile a cheeky challenge.

'Isn't cooking a part of every modern bachelor's repertoire?'

'Not that I've noticed.' She unsnapped her seat belt. 'The odd fellow might manage to barbecue sausages to a delicate shade of black, but that's about it. And you mentioned exotic ingredients. I'm impressed.' Leaning over, she kissed Sam. It was a playful, teasing kiss full on his lips.

And it was all that it took to *completely* change his focus.

Now wasn't the time to admit that he had only practised and perfected one recipe and that, after that, he was back to opening cans of beans. Instead, he trapped her lovely face between his hands and returned her kiss. The gear stick was a bit of a problem and they were both grinning, so their teeth collided a little, which meant it wasn't an award-winning kiss.

But it didn't matter. Hell, nothing seemed to matter when Meg was this close. This tempting.

She pulled away, giggling. 'If we hurry with our exotic shopping, we should still be able to catch the next boat.'

'OK. Now, where's a good seafood shop? I need crayfish, king prawns, scallops...'

As they made their way around the shopping centre unearthing Sam's ingredients, Meg tried to ignore the way her common sense kept pricking her. She didn't want to be reminded that this sudden flash rerun of yesterday's happy, charming Sam wouldn't last.

Any minute now, he could become reabsorbed in his problems. She decided the best she could do was make the most of this time out. Perhaps the story of Dolly and Tom's brief love had taught her a lesson? To seize the day? The hour? The moment?

The way she felt about Sam was so surprising. She had never expected to become so smitten by a man she'd only just met.

And she had certainly never expected to feel so ecstatically happy searching for udon noodles, baby bok choy or oyster mushrooms. The intensity of her feelings bubbled through her as if her veins had been filled with soda pop. There could only be one explanation. The same one she'd arrived at last night. She loved Sam. Loved him, loved him, loved him.

She hadn't been looking for love. It had just leaped into her life without knocking first. And, while Sam hadn't actually mentioned love, he'd told her that he'd never felt this way before either. Knowing that, felt good.

His smiling eyes met hers through a carefully stacked display of pumpkin-soup tins and a delicious, joyful shiver skittered over her. She felt like dancing a jig down the aisles. She sure hoped Sam didn't intend to spend too much time in the kitchen. She had other plans for this evening.

Last night's lovemaking had left her with an incredibly desperate need for more.

'All I need now is ginger and soy sauce,' he said.

'All I need is another kiss.'

A smile tugged at his lips. 'Come here, then.' He pulled her behind the tins of soup and, ducking his head, kissed her soundly on the mouth. 'How much time do we have?' He growled the words, nuzzling her neck just below her ear. 'I hadn't realised shopping was so seductive.'

She couldn't help grinning as she glanced at her wristwatch. 'We should just make the boat.'

There was a dreamlike quality to their happiness as they rushed through the checkout and sped back to the ferry terminal.

The only man who'd ever cooked for Meg had been her father. She loved the idea that Sam wanted to impress her with his skills in something as domestic as cooking.

She could visualise everything. She would tuck a tea towel around his waist, turn her stereo on and pour two glasses of wine.

Sitting on the end of the bench, she would admire the

way he chopped and sautéed. No doubt they would exchange quick, cheeky kisses whenever he came near her. They'd be laughing and joking…

And then, afterwards…

On the ferry, they sat outside on the upper deck, close together, while the wind and the sea rushed and slapped noisily about them. It was hard to talk. The ends of sentences were whipped away by the wind, so they smiled at each other instead. And they touched in deceptively casual little ways—a hand resting on a shoulder or a knee—a nose brushed against a cheek—lips against hair.

Each touch, each look set off flash points of longing so that it took all Meg's self-control not to throw her arms around Sam and make a public spectacle of herself.

On the island once more, Sam loaded the shopping into the back of the Moke, while Meg slipped into the driver's seat. All she could think about was being alone with him again. She was frustrated by the length of time it took to negotiate the narrow road to the resort. It followed a series of hills and valleys as it wound its way over headlands and skimmed along the flat edges of palm fringed bays. Finally, they chugged into the driveway of Magnetic Rendezvous.

'I'd like to pick up my laptop before I come to your place,' Sam said. 'At some stage, I need to send some e-mail messages back to Seattle.'

'OK,' Meg replied, trying to sound offhand about the fact that he could think about business right now when all she could think of was kissing him and touching him.

Sam captured her hand and swung her towards him. 'I'll see you in five,' he murmured. 'Don't go away. I'm going to need some help in the kitchen.' He rubbed his thumb gently over her lower lip and smiled slowly, his eyes trapping hers—making every pulse in her body throb. His mouth dipped to tease hers. 'Actually, any old room will do, but I'm going to need you there, Meg.'

She felt the flames leap into her cheeks and she couldn't reply. There was no way she could talk. She wasn't even sure she was still breathing. A feverish longing was eating her up. In a daze, she hurried to her cottage and shoved the seafood into the fridge. Her senses on high alert for the sound of Sam's footsteps, she hurried into the bathroom and cleaned her teeth.

She had never felt so fired up, so highly sensitised, so tingling with expectation. So hot! She was smouldering with such wild thoughts, there was every chance that, when Sam walked through her doorway, she would shock the socks off him.

When her phone rang, she ignored it. There was no way she could carry on a normal conversation with anyone right now. She checked her watch. Five minutes he'd said. Well, it was bordering on five minutes now.

Meg tried to calm down. She strode through to her kitchen and filled a glass with water. As she drank it, she closed her eyes and willed herself to relax.

Sam's phone rang just as he was heading for the door with his laptop under one arm. He grabbed the door frame for balance as he stopped abruptly and scowled at the squat little phone sitting on his coffee table. It continued its insistent ringing. Damn it! He knew a telephone could be annoying but, now, when he was on his way to Meg, it was an instrument of torture. Slamming his palm against the door frame, he hovered for another second, then stepped outside and shoved his door closed behind him.

Whoever was calling could wait.

*   *   *

Meg glimpsed Sam's profile as he strode past her kitchen window. Then she saw the back of his tanned neck and the neat line of his hair before he disappeared around the corner of the cottage. By the time he reached her front door, the slim laptop at his side, she was there too. He grinned, bent down and kissed her cheek.

'I missed you,' she whispered.

For a moment, he leaned away from her to deposit the laptop carefully on her dining table but, when he straightened, he reached to her, hauling her close. 'I'm here to stay.' His smiling gaze linked to hers. 'You know, those eyes of yours give you away every time.'

'What colour are they now?' she asked.

'Sweetheart, I'm not talking about their colour.' His kiss was hot and hard and Meg couldn't hold back her soft sighs of pleasure.

The telephone rang again.

'Damn phone,' Sam muttered against her mouth as he deepened the kiss. Her arms rose to entwine around his neck but, as the sound from the kitchen persisted, he groaned.

Reluctantly, Meg dragged her lips from his. 'There was someone ringing here earlier, but I'm afraid I ignored it,' she admitted.

'I had a call that I didn't answer, too.' Sam glared at the phone.

'Pity I don't have an answering machine.'

'I wonder if they'll keep trying all evening?'

'Best get rid of whoever it is.' With a heavy, regret-laden sigh, Meg released her hold on his neck.

'You want me to take it?' Sam asked.

'Thanks.'

She watched as Sam snatched up the receiver. After grunting his name, he listened in silence. A silence that went on way too long.

CHAPTER SIX

MEG watched as Sam stood with one hand propped against the kitchen wall and listened intently to the caller. He stared down at the white tiled floor and shook his head. 'There's got to be some mistake!'

Oh, no, she thought and her stomach clenched. What's gone wrong? She took a tentative step closer.

'There's got to be a record somewhere.' Sam yelled into the phone and she heard a note of rising frustration in his voice. His eyes closed as he concentrated hard on whatever his caller was saying. He nodded as he listened in agitated silence. 'OK. OK,' he said at last. 'Yeah. I met her. She has a certificate. Yes, yes, I'll get back just as soon as I can.' He pressed the disconnect button and dropped the phone before covering his face with his hands.

Meg's heart leaped wildly. 'What's happened?'

His head snapped up. His eyes were so fierce they'd darkened to navy. 'Our lawyers can't find a wedding certificate for my grandparents.'

'You mean, there's no record at all?'

'Sweet nothing.'

'So that means—'

'It means that almost certainly my grandparents were never married.' Sam shot a warning glance in her direction. 'Don't you start on about how happy you are for Dolly.'

Meg gasped. 'Well, I guess I am pleased for Dolly.' She took another step towards him. 'But I can understand your family's problems as well. This is awful for you. Are they going to keep looking, or are the lawyers certain there's nothing to be found?'

'They'll probably make a few more investigations. But there's virtually no hope,' he told her bluntly. With a despondent sigh, he shoved his hands deep in the pockets of his jeans.' They've already done an exhaustive search. It looks as if my grandmother's family did a cover-up job about the marriage. She and Tom Kirby were already engaged before he left—and she was pregnant. Somehow, I doubt Tom knew that.'

'But they never married?'

'No. My grandmother came from old blue-blood stock. Her family would have hated the stigma of illegitimacy.'

'I'm so sorry. This must be a terrible blow for you.'

'Yeah. It looks like Dolly was right all along. The letter was meant for her.' He pulled his hands back out of his pockets and banged one knuckled fist against the other. 'Which means Dolly is probably the legal inheritor of Kirby & Son.'

'Goodness.' Meg cried. 'Where does that put you and your family?'

His mouth stretched into a grimacing grin as he shook his head. 'Into a long, expensive, legal mess that could go on for years.'

'How terrible.' A feeling of dread swept through Meg. She hurried to Sam's side and gave him what she hoped was a reassuring hug. In return, he dropped a swift kiss on her cheek, but she could see his mind was distracted elsewhere.

'It looks like this whole business of coming over here to Australia for the bottle—has caused a huge problem for you and your family,' she said in a flat tone that matched the sinking feeling in her stomach.

He heaved a loud sigh. 'It sure has.'

The room seemed to sway abruptly. Meg reached for the back of a nearby chair to steady herself. What else had she expected Sam to say? That it didn't matter? That finding her had been the highlight of his life? That one night with her cancelled out the down side of losing millions of dollars, a family company and his father's legitimacy?

She willed the walls to stop closing in.

Sam spoke again. 'Of course, my lawyers will still want to take a good look at the letter. Nothing's certain until that's been sighted. That reminds me—' Abruptly, he picked up the phone again. 'Reception?' He barked the word. 'Sam Kirby here. I need to advance my return flight to Seattle. Can you organise that for me? That's right. I need the first available flight back. You've got my details, haven't you?'

As he replaced the phone, Meg stared at him open-mouthed. She had known this news meant Sam would have to go home, but so soon? 'You're going back, just like that? Straight away?'

'I have to get back. You can see that, can't you?'

'Yes,' she said in a cold little voice. 'After all, there's a lot of money at stake.'

His jaw clenched. 'You really have got a huge chip on your shoulder when it comes to money, haven't you?' He glared at her and his shoulders stiffened.

Her stomach churned as she watched him pace the room, his face dark and grim.

'You don't realise what's *really* at stake here.' He hurled the words at her angrily. 'It's not just about money. Four generations of my family have worked hard to build up a fine, successful company. I've worked my butt off to keep it going since my father took sick. And now, it could all be lost. It's unbelievable that we could lose it just because—'

He plunged tense fingers into his hair. 'I'm still not sure this isn't some kind of incredible prank. If I take my lawyers' advice, everything should be under suspicion. Dolly's story is so hard to believe.'

Meg frowned at him. 'But Dolly has proof.'

He crossed his arms over his chest and she averted her eyes. The pose made his physique more impressive than ever. But her drooling days were over.

'We don't know yet if any of her papers are legitimate,' he said coldly. 'Anyone can mock up photos and certificates these days.'

Meg stared at Sam, aghast. 'Dolly wouldn't. How can you even suggest such a thing? You've got to be wrong about that.'

This was too much!

She thought of the smile she and Dolly had shared— the smile of one woman in love recognising the same blinding joy in the other. 'I'm sure you're wrong, Sam. You can't possibly believe it.'

'It wouldn't be the first time people have been hoodwinked by white hair and a sweet smile.'

Meg tried to suppress a growing suspicion that she'd been hoodwinked by blue eyes and a sexy smile. While she watched, Sam seemed to be transforming from a sensitive, exquisite lover into a hard-bitten, callous sceptic.

'Sam,' she said, deliberately keeping her tone sympathetic. 'I can understand how upset you must be by all this. But can't you believe Dolly's story? Can't you imagine how it was for Tom and her? Meeting here, just as we have, and falling helplessly in love?' Her voice broke on the word 'love.'

For a brief moment, his eyes linked to hers and their

flinty hardness softened. His Adam's apple moved up and down in his throat.

Please, Sam, she begged silently. *Please tell me you can picture what love was like for them.* Surely, if he felt only half the emotion she was feeling for him, he would know Dolly's story made sense.

But his next chilling words proved to her that he was on a completely different wavelength. 'Everything about this whole situation stinks. Look at the way Fred's used me to get his grubby publicity. Honestly, right now, I can't help thinking the whole business with the bottle and the letter has all been one huge hoax.'

Stunned, she backed away from him until she bumped into her sofa. She sank into it as his words echoed in her head. *One huge hoax? He didn't believe she'd found the bottle!* How could Sam doubt her? Last night he'd thanked her for finding it in front of a resort full of people.

And he'd given every impression that he was falling in love with her.

He had made perfect, beautiful love to her!

Tears slid down her face and she let them fall.

No wonder Sam hadn't trusted Dolly. He didn't trust anyone! For Pete's sake! When he'd first come to the island, he'd hidden his real identity. He'd been suspicious of her right from the start!

This was beyond terrible! Meg had never felt so wretched—as if she had fallen into a swirling black whirlpool and was drowning... She struggled to breathe.

Sam stopped pacing. His mind had been seething with shock and a hundred worries, but suddenly it penetrated that Meg had been silent for a long time. He blinked and looked around searching for her.

She was curled up on the sofa, her lovely, honey-tanned legs tucked primly to one side and her curls tumbling every which way around her face. He peered closer. Her face looked blotchy, streaked and strained. Concerned, he walked over to her and touched her cheek.

If she hadn't seemed so stiff and tense he would have stooped to kiss her, but something in the tight, held-in way she was sitting stopped him. 'Are you OK, Meg?'

Her answer was to haul herself off the sofa and to storm out to the kitchen. 'I'm getting extremely hungry.' She tossed the words over her shoulder. 'But I don't suppose you'll have time to cook dinner now.'

'Er—I guess that depends on what flights are available.' From the kitchen, he could hear the sounds of Meg opening the door of the refrigerator. 'Meg, I've been so agitated. I might have said something out of turn. I don't even know now what I said. I—'

Her hard voice interrupted him. 'Nice try, Sam, but don't expect me to buy it.'

He frowned. He still couldn't see Meg's face. She was hunting around in a cupboard for something, but she was sounding as edgy as a precipice.

Completely baffled, he offered an apologetic smile in her direction. 'I take it you're mad at me?'

Her head came out of a cupboard and she glared at him, her face flushed. 'I think you'd better take your seafood and your computer and get out of here,' she said slowly, her tone icily quiet.

Struggling to make sense of her anger, he held his hands out in a gesture of innocence. 'Don't I get any kind of explanation?'

Shaking her head, Meg folded her arms across her chest and looked away. He could have sworn her chin was trembling as if she were struggling to hold back tears. His heart lurched. 'Meg,' he shouted angrily. 'Speak to me.'

She almost—*almost*—weakened. Turning her tear-blurred eyes back to Sam, Meg saw his genuinely puzzled expression, as if he was honestly confused. It was tempting to simply throw herself into his arms, to have a sob that he could kiss better and to forget what he had just said about the bottle being a hoax.

But that was the weak option and she'd been weak around Sam Kirby just once too often. She'd given in to the ultimate weakness with a man she hardly knew.

Drawing in a deep, strengthening breath and then releasing it once more, she said softly, so softly she wondered if he could hear her, 'When we made love, I was offering you more than my body.'

She saw him stiffen. His face tightened, his shoulders straightened and he seemed to grow taller. 'Yes?'

'I told you I'm not in the habit of—of sleeping around.'

'Meg, I didn't think for one moment—What are you trying to tell me?'

'I have to feel emotionally involved with a man. I *did* feel very emotionally involved with you, Sam.'

His throat worked and he stared at her, his eyes puzzled. She wanted to tell him how she'd fallen head over heels for him—that already she loved him deeply, irrevocably. But it was way too late for that kind of admission.

'I *trusted* you.'

'Of course you can trust me, Meg.'

Tears threatened, but she willed herself not to cry. 'Trust has to be mutual.'

Sam's hands rose to his hips. He shook his head. 'Meg, I'm no good at guessing. This is driving me insane.' At that moment, the phone rang again and he snatched it up. 'Kirby.'

Meg's heart thumped and crashed harder than ever as she watched him listen carefully to his caller.

'That's good,' he answered with a grim nod of his head. 'Thanks. I'll be there soon.'

His eyes swung to Meg and she felt herself grow cold. 'They can get you a seat on a flight out *tonight*?' Couldn't he at least stay tonight? Just one more night?

'Yeah. I can get a flight out of Townsville to Sydney. That way I can catch the first connection to the US in the morning.'

'That's—that's what you want, isn't it?' Meg felt on the edge of panic. They were fighting. But that didn't stop her from wanting him. That didn't stop her from feeling desolate because Sam didn't need her the way she needed him.

He took a step towards her and reached out to touch her arm. 'What can I say to make amends?'

'Don't bother,' she cried and she made a dismissive gesture with her hand.

His eyes narrowed. 'What if I want to bother? What if I don't want to leave here with things in a mess like this?'

She shook her head, trying to convince herself that she wanted Sam out of her life. It was the only sensible way to handle this. She'd broken her own wise rule. She'd fallen in love with a resort guest.

And now she was paying the price.

She knew from the experience of her friends that once a man left the island he wanted to forget any romantic entanglements.

Looking straight at him, she said, 'You're—you're very—attractive, Sam Kirby, and it will probably take me twenty light years to forget about—last night.' She pressed her lips together tightly and took another breath before adding softly, 'But I can't trust my feelings right now.' Her eyes met his and she didn't look away as she added, 'And you're not thinking straight either. I'm afraid if I listen to anything else you try to say now I'll end up in a terrible mess.'

A wave of self-disgust clenched Sam's stomach. How could he have been such an A-grade ass? He had always prided himself on his diplomacy and now he struggled to place exactly where everything had started going wrong. How had he made such a royal mess of things?

Meg wasn't a girl who made love lightly. Intuitively, he had known that. In a way it had been part of why he'd found her so alluring.

Grimacing, he shoved his hands deep in his pockets. He had a fair idea he knew what was at the bottom of her hurt feelings. 'Meg, we aren't the same as Tom and Dolly.'

A weird little sob came from her direction. 'How do you mean?'

'They had a whirlwind romance and jumped straight into a hasty marriage.'

'Don't be silly. I don't expect you to marry me.'

He looked at her carefully, trying to guess if he was missing any subtleties of meaning here. 'It was different for them,' he suggested gently. 'They were in the middle of a war. Tom knew that any day he might die.'

'Of course, Sam, you don't have to—'

'Listen!' he ordered, his tension breaking through. 'I'm not saying that what I feel for you isn't just as strong. But our circumstances are completely different. We've had even less time to get to know each other than they had. I guess I should have known better than to—'

'I understand!' Meg cried. 'You don't have to spell out the fact that we both made a hasty mistake.'

He sighed. The way things stood, he really had no choice but to leave tonight. 'I'd really like to hang around and sort this out. But my company's in the middle of all kinds of hassles back home. Not just this latest crisis. My father's ill, so I have to get back to cushion the blow of this news for him. I'm not in a position to even think about the long term.'

She said through her teeth, 'I don't need a list of your explanations. I'm sorry things are so bad for you. I don't want to make it worse. Please, just go.'

'It'll take me quite a while to stop thinking about you, too, Meg.'

She gave him a look that said loudly and clearly that she didn't believe him.

'As soon as I've sorted everything out I'll come back.'

'Don't try to make me feel better, Sam. And, please, don't make promises you can't keep.'

'I want to come back and get to know you properly, Meg. I'll write to you.' He struggled to find a way to lighten the moment. 'But I do getting-to-know-you best face to face.'

She bit her lip, but he was rewarded by the tiniest chink of a wayward smile. 'Of course you do,' she said. 'You're even better at mouth-to-mouth.' She held up her hands as if to ward him off. 'That's the trouble with you, Sam Kirby.'

'I'll be back for sure next year for that coral-spawning you were telling me about. I can't miss out on the world's biggest sexual encounter.' He crossed the room and leaned down quickly to steal one final taste of her warm lips.

He felt her mouth tremble beneath his and heard the sharp intake of her breath.

'I'll be seeing you, Nutmeg,' he whispered. He wasn't feeling very cheerful, but he managed to wink at her.

Meg watched Sam disappear into the night and felt an enormous wave of hopeless misery wash cruelly over her. Her face crumpled as the tears began again. She tried to tell herself she had no right to feel so let down. She was being foolish.

All along she had known that Sam had only wanted a holiday romance. It was why she'd tried so hard to resist him. But last night, she'd honestly felt he cared for her in a way that went way beyond casual sex. She'd been quite certain she wasn't just another notch on a playboy bachelor's bedpost.

Now she was just as sure she'd been wrong. Sam might think he cared for her. But he couldn't have let fly with that hurtful remark about the bottle if he felt the way she did. It was clear that he didn't feel the same helplessness, the same sense of spinning out of control, the same all-consuming need that was eating her up.

Once he got home to Seattle—to his business, his family and his girlfriends—he would be like all the rest. He would soon forget this brief holiday affair.

Shivering, she wandered into the kitchen, dragged the bag of seafood out of her fridge, and, with an angry cry, tossed it into the freezer compartment.

So much for the romantic dinner!

How could she ever have imagined her destiny was linked to that stupid bottle?

And what in the world was she going to do about her feelings for Sam?

CHAPTER SEVEN

'SAM, darling, how lovely to see you.' Amanda Kirby beamed at her son as he strode into the familiar kitchen of his parents' waterfront home on the outskirts of Seattle. 'I was just going to make your father a cup of coffee. I'll bring a cup for you, too. Go find him. He's out on the deck. It's lovely this morning in the sunshine.'

Sam kissed his mother's cheek. 'I'll hang around in here while you make the coffee. Then we can go out together.'

Amanda sent Sam several thoughtful glances over her shoulder as she filled the coffee maker, selected cups and saucers and placed them on a tray. 'Are you keeping well, son?'

'Sure,' he replied quickly. 'Hey, don't rush straight into mother mode. I've only been here a minute.'

'I'm sorry. But you must be used to my fussing by now. It's just that, ever since you came back from Australia, you seem…strained. And you're looking thinner I'm sure.'

'I'm fine.' Sam watched in silence as his mother poured cream into a delicate porcelain jug and selected coffee spoons. 'I do have a few things weighing on my mind,' he admitted at last.

'I know that, dear.' Amanda crossed the room to where he stood leaning against the pantry cupboard and gave him a hearty, motherly hug. 'Would one of these things on your mind be a pretty blonde Australian girl?'

He eyed his mother shrewdly and released a half-sigh,

half-laugh. 'I heard that some photos found their way back here, but I didn't think you read those sorts of magazines.'

'I don't, but my cleaning lady does. She showed them to me. You seemed—er—quite taken with the young lady.'

Sam grimaced. His mother didn't usually comment about his appearances in the press. She was used to it. 'They caught me at an unguarded moment.'

'Several unguarded moments.'

His head jerked up. 'How many photos have you seen?' Then, shoving his hands in his pockets, he added quickly, 'Don't answer that. I'd rather not know.'

'She looks like a lovely young woman.'

'It's nothing serious,' he muttered, determined not to discuss Meg with his mother. 'You know how the press get carried away.'

'It's high time you did get serious about a girl. I don't know how your lady friends put up with your casual attitude.' Amanda stepped a pace away from her son and eyed him shrewdly. 'Julia Davenport seemed to miss you while you were away.'

Sam scowled. But his mind raced ahead. If he didn't make a quick response to this not-so-subtle hint, his mother would launch full steam ahead with another of her matchmaking ploys. 'I'm taking Julia to the theatre next week,' he said hastily. He'd have to remember to get Ellen to arrange that.

Amanda brightened. 'That will be lovely. What are you going to see?'

'Er…Julia's making the selection.'

She looked even more pleased. 'Julia has excellent taste. She's very knowledgeable about the arts.'

'I hope she chooses a comedy. I could do with some

lightening up. Look,' he said with a sigh, 'there's something completely different and much more important I want to talk to you about.' He paused for a beat or two. 'I have some bad news for Dad.'

Amanda frowned. 'How bad?'

'Bad enough that I think I should tell you first and you can see whether you think he can take it.'

'Oh, heavens, Sam.'

'It's about the will. The will in the bottle.'

'I must say, I've been very curious about that.'

'It wasn't meant for us.'

'Why ever not?'

Sam looked away from his mother's anxious eyes. 'It was written for Tom Kirby's wife.'

'Judith? But she was your father's mother—*your* grandmother.'

'No. Mother,' he said quietly. 'Not Judith.'

Amanda's face paled. 'But that's ridiculous.' She raised a shaking hand to her mouth. 'You don't mean…?' Grabbing her son's arm, she shook him. 'What on earth are you saying?'

He told her about Tom and Dolly and his grandmother's cover-up.

For several long, shocked minutes, Amanda Kirby stood perfectly still in the middle of her beautiful designer kitchen. Sam could see by her increasingly stricken expression that the full implication of his news was slowly sinking in—his father's illegitimacy and the threat to the Kirby family's holdings.

After some time, he said, 'One piece of good news is that Dolly Kirby isn't interested in any part of the family business, although legally she could lay claim to everything.'

Amanda nodded, her dark brown eyes wide in her still pale face.

'She says she hasn't contributed anything to Kirby & Son and she doesn't expect anything in return…except the acknowledged legitimacy of her marriage by this family.'

'This family? By that, you mean all of us? Including your father?'

Sam nodded.

Amanda walked unsteadily back to the stove. After a long moment of silence she said, 'There's no way I could keep a secret like that to myself…and your father's been much better lately. I think he can take this news.' She turned and shot Sam a warning glance. 'But we'll have to find a careful way to put it to him.'

'OK. I'll follow your lead.' Sam took the laden tray from his mother. 'And there's one other thing I'd like to discuss with Dad as soon as possible. It's to do with the business.'

Amanda frowned. 'Can we take this one step at a time?'

Meg watched the doctor's expression, trying to read her thoughts. Eventually, she said, 'Yes, my dear, you're pregnant. There's no doubt about it.'

Meg closed her eyes as alarm mingled with excitement. So it was true!

It was a shock, but not exactly unexpected. Over the past month, she'd experienced all the well-known symptoms of pregnancy and the kit she'd bought from the chemist had produced a positive result. But hearing the doctor's confirmation made it so definite.

Pregnant!

A tiny new life growing inside her.

The female doctor studied Meg over her half-glasses. 'Is this good news?'

Meg opened her mouth to answer and then hesitated. Was it good news? She couldn't tell. Couldn't think. The only thought that stayed steady in her head was that, now, she would never be able to forget Sam.

'Meg? Are you all right, dear?'

Startled, she looked at the doctor and realised she was expected to say something. 'I'm sorry,' she murmured. 'What did you ask me? We definitely used protection. It must have failed. I don't know how it failed.'

'Unfortunately, these things still happen.' The doctor sighed and reached out to give Meg's hand a reassuring pat. 'But don't worry. You're a strong, healthy young woman. You'll breeze through this pregnancy and, at the end of it, there'll be a beautiful baby.'

Meg nodded and attempted to smile, but her lips and smile muscles wouldn't respond. This was supposed to be a special moment. She should be rushing home to her husband to share the good news. That was how she'd always imagined news of such an event would happen.

Her handsome husband would be thrilled. He'd tell her to take it easy…and then he'd place his hand lovingly on her stomach…and he'd offer to bring her a cup of tea in bed in the mornings…

Now, she realised that a picture like that was only a silly, girlish dream. This was reality. She looked at the doctor. 'I was hoping to be able to pick up my postgrad studies next term.'

'That still might be possible,' the doctor said thoughtfully, but she sounded doubtful.

Meg dropped her head into her hands. No Sam…no marine science…just a baby… She felt so tired, so overwhelmed.

'Meg?' The doctor's voice sounded sterner and louder. 'You do plan to go ahead with the pregnancy, don't you?'

'Oh, yes.' She dragged her thoughts back to the present, to this room with its sensible carpet and the smell of medicine and the doctor sitting at her desk looking ultra neat and sensible. And concerned. 'I wouldn't consider— No, I definitely want to have this baby.'

'Good. That's settled, then.'

Now that she'd said the words out loud—*I definitely want to have this baby*—Meg felt a whole heap better. 'When is my baby due?' she asked. *My baby.* How strange those two words sounded.

The doctor consulted her chart. 'Going by your dates, I'd say somewhere around the middle of February.'

'February,' Meg repeated. Summer. The island was usually at its hottest and wettest in February. It was right in the middle of the wet season. Not the best time of the year to have a baby.

'We'll get a clearer idea of how far along you are when we see the ultrasound pictures in a few weeks' time.'

Meg nodded.

Glancing at Meg's ringless left hand, the doctor added, 'Do you have a partner to support you?'

'No.' Her mind flashed to what Sam had said about whirlwind romances and hasty commitments. *I'm not in a position to even think about the long term.* When she saw the other woman's faint frown, she added, 'But I'm OK. I'm fine.'

'What about your family?'

Again Meg shook her head. 'I'm afraid there's just me.' She tried to flash a bright, confident smile, but she knew the doctor wasn't fooled. 'I'll manage quite well,' she said more boldly. 'My father died earlier this year, but he left me enough to manage for the time being.'

A sudden vision of her father swam into her imagination and Meg was engulfed by a wave of sadness. Dad wouldn't see this little baby—his grandchild.

Just as Sam won't see his son or daughter, another thought whispered. She pressed the heels of her hands against her eyes.

'I'm sorry,' the doctor said gently. 'It's tough doing this on your own.'

'I'm just missing—' a sob escaped '—missing Dad.'

'Of course. And you'll find you're inclined to be a little weepy for a while. You can put it down to hormones.' After a sympathetic pause, she went on to outline some of the more routine aspects of monitoring a pregnancy and she gave Meg a pamphlet about pregnancy support groups. Eventually the visit was over.

Back out on the street, Meg was crossing the car park to her Mini Moke when the upside of her situation suddenly hit her. A baby meant that she would be part of a family again. A twosome. Mother and child. She and her baby would be close—just as she'd been with her father. She'd have someone to love her again. Someone for her to love back.

The thought of a baby's soft chubby arms clasping her made her smile as she turned the key in the ignition. She allowed herself to dream a little.

Maybe the baby would be a boy. A little boy with short black hair and sky-blue eyes. She could picture his cute, cheeky grin. Like Sam's.

That thought brought another painful block of tears damming her throat. *No, she didn't miss Sam Kirby!*

She wouldn't be able to tell him about the baby. Not after the way they'd parted. What could he do besides give her money? She didn't want his money and she certainly didn't want him directing her life, from the other side of the Pacific.

As if thinking about Sam today wasn't misery enough, there was a parcel from him when she got home. With fumbling fingers, Meg opened it and, nestling in a velvet-lined silver box was a beautiful Ceylon-blue sapphire pendant on a silver chain.

He had written a note on the accompanying card in funny, square handwriting: 'As soon as I can, I want to see how your eyes catch its blue sparkle.'

'Oh, Sam,' Meg whispered and began to sob at once.

Even from such a distance he could reach the most vulnerable corners of her heart. With very little effort, Sam could show up her weakness. Whatever he did made her want him. She was having his baby! What on earth was she going to do?

Sinking onto a chair, she clutched the pendant and raised her hands to cover her face. She could feel the cool stone pressing into her hot cheek and a miserable shudder shook her body.

Meg didn't know how long she huddled there weeping, but after a time the flow slowed to a trickle and a persistent thought kept nudging her attention. She *should* let Sam know about the baby. Part of her desperately wanted to tell him. Not that she thought for one moment that he would be pleased with the news. It would just be another complication in his already complicated life.

But it was *his* baby. She could reassure him that she was fine and she could insist that she didn't need anything. But she would feel better if he knew.

Frowning thoughtfully, she dug her diary out of her handbag and found the page that listed the various time zones.

*   *   *

And just before seven the next morning, she nervously punched in the numbers Sam had left her.

Her hand shook and her throat felt parched as she held the receiver to her ear. It took a few minutes for her to be put through from the main Kirby & Son office to Sam's personal assistant. Of course, it would have been expecting too much to think he had given her the number of his direct line.

'Sam Kirby's office. How can I help you?' asked a pleasant female voice.

'Oh.' Meg swallowed back a sudden surge of panic. 'Could I speak to Mr Kirby, please?'

'I'm afraid he's busy at a meeting right now. Who's speaking?'

'Ah—my name's Meg Bennet. Sam—um—has my number.'

'Meg Bennet!' the other woman cried and Meg was stunned by the rush of warmth and excitement in her voice. 'Oh, Meg, I'm so sorry. Sam is going to be tied up in meetings all afternoon. Perhaps you should try him at home this evening. Just let me check his diary and I'll see what he's doing tonight.'

Meg heard the sound of pages rustling. Then she heard what definitely sounded like a sigh on the other end of the line.

'Oh, dear,' Sam's assistant said. 'He does have something pencilled in for this evening. But if you ring around six, you should be able to catch him before he goes out.'

A wave of nausea almost prevented Meg from answering. Sam hadn't given her his home number, but this woman assumed she would know it.

'Is there any other way I can help you?' came the friendly voice again.

'Could you—I don't have—I seem to have lost Sam's

home number.' Feeling more embarrassed than ever, Meg asked, 'Could you give it to me, please?'

'Of course, dear. You *must* have Sam's home number.'

Slightly puzzled by the surprising friendliness of the woman's tone, Meg copied down the digits. But after the call disconnected, she sank into another depressed huddle on her sofa.

All night, she'd lain awake thinking about making this call. She'd practised a dozen different ways to tell Sam her news. *I'm pregnant. I'm going to have a baby. Your baby. You're going to have a baby. We're going to have a baby. When's Father's Day in America?*

She'd been so pent up with nerves, she'd almost chickened out of ringing him at all! And now she had to wait for several more hours!

Perhaps she wasn't strong enough for this.

Being distracted by work all morning helped, so she was feeling more relaxed at the beginning of her lunch hour, when she hurried back to her cottage to make an attempt at calling him at home.

But her relaxation evaporated when a young woman answered.

'Sam's place.' She purred the words. 'Julia speaking.'

'I—I—Could I please speak to Sam?' Oh, Lord! She panicked. A girlfriend! Do I have to tell him he's about to become a father, when there's another woman standing right beside him? She almost slammed the receiver down.

'Who's speaking?' the woman asked and the question sounded as if it had been dipped in ice.

Meg pressed her forehead with a damp palm. 'Meg. Meg Bennet. From North Queensland. Australia.' Her heart was thumping so loudly she wondered if it was echoing down the airwaves.

There was a distinct pause. 'I'm afraid Sam's busy

right now. He's taking a shower.' Another pause. 'But, as you're calling long distance, would you like me to take the phone through to him?'

'No!' Meg cried, and she cringed as she realised it was more like a scream. 'No,' she repeated in a whisper. 'I'll—I'll try again some other time. Goodbye.'

She crashed the receiver down and slumped against the wall, a hand pressed against her pounding chest. Sam had a girlfriend, who could casually talk about walking in on him in the shower without turning a hair!

She closed her eyes and tried to block out the images that thought conjured. She knew he was a handsome bachelor millionaire. Of course a cavalcade of *intimate* girlfriends went with the territory.

Why hadn't she expected something like this? Sam might have told Meg she was special. He might have thought he meant it at the time. But hearing that silky, sophisticated voice reinforced for Meg something she had known all along: Men put island holiday romances completely out of their minds as soon as they reached home.

She felt more miserable and alone than ever. If Sam wanted to forget about her, she'd give him every chance. And she would have to do her best to forget about him, too.

There was really only one way...

Still fastening his cufflinks, Sam walked into his lounge to fix himself a quick drink before Julia Davenport arrived. He needed a stiff one before he faced the evening ahead. Julia was pleasant enough company but, since he'd come home from Australia, his interest in women had lost its punch.

Perhaps it had been the intoxicating effects of the tropical sea air but, whenever he looked at another woman these days, visions of Meg seemed to haunt him.

Picking up a decanter, he glimpsed a slight movement in his peripheral vision. He double checked. Julia was sitting on his sofa, dressed in something black and skimpy. One long leg was elegantly crossed over the other and a long slender arm was draped along the back of the sofa.

Now she uncurled herself slowly, like a lazy cat.

'Julia. I didn't realise you were already here.'

'I let myself in,' she said in a sultry croon as she glided across the room towards him.

'How?' he asked, puzzled.

She smiled from beneath lowered lashes. 'Your mother gave me a key while you were away. So I could water your house plants.'

Sam's jaw clenched. 'I have a maid who attends to the house plants. My mother knows that.' He poured himself a doubly stiff Scotch.

'Sam.' Julia pouted. 'Don't be angry with me. I thought it would be good if I was more—*available*.'

He ignored her innuendo. 'There was a phone ringing earlier. Did you take it?'

A dark scowl clouded her face, undoing the effects of her carefully applied make-up. She flicked her head and said airily, 'It was just a wrong number.'

Had he imagined that slight shiftiness in her eyes as she'd answered? Sam downed his drink in an angry gulp. If Julia thought he wanted her to be available, she was in for a disappointing night.

The following week, Ellen brought Sam's mail through to his office and, instead of quietly placing it at one end of his desk and leaving again without disturbing him, she stood, holding a small square parcel and tapping it with a fingernail.

'This looks familiar,' she intoned darkly.

Sam jerked his attention away from the figures he was analysing. 'What's that?'

'This parcel looks remarkably like something you asked me to post a couple of weeks ago and it has Australian stamps.' She handed it to him.

A pulse in Sam's neck began to beat as he jumped to his feet. 'Thanks, Ellen.'

He waited till she'd gone before he opened it. With a sickening sense of foreboding, he ripped the paper off the package. Inside was a polite little note from Meg and the sapphire pendant he'd sent her, carefully boxed and re-wrapped!

He sank into a chair as he read and reread her note. Short and to the point, it covered the basic courtesies and managed to politely refuse his gift without any proper explanation. It was as impersonal as a bank statement.

It was a savage slap in the face!

With an angry cry, Sam tossed the note and its lilac-coloured envelope onto his desk and charged across the room. He hurt like hell! And the pain wasn't merely the smarting of a bruised ego.

Damn it! He really liked Meg. He liked her a lot. Maybe more than a lot. If he wasn't so tied up with this business, he'd be back there now finding out exactly *how* he felt about her.

Checking his watch, he calculated the differences between the time zones in Seattle and eastern Australia, reached for the phone on his desk and dialled.

When Fred Raynor grumbled into the phone, Sam asked to be put through to Meg.

'She's not here.' Fred barked the words out.

'Is she on leave?'

'No, mate. Resigned. She left last week. Just handed in her notice and took off.'

Sam felt as if he'd been hurled from a plane without a parachute. 'Why?' he managed to croak.

'Can't help you, mate. I wouldn't have a flaming clue.'

'Do you know where she went?'

'Haven't the foggiest idea. She didn't leave a forwarding address. You can't trust staff to hang around these days! No sense of loyalty.'

After hanging up, Sam snatched up the packaging and checked the postmark. It had been posted from the island just over a week ago. He scoured everything she'd sent, looking for a return address, but there was none.

Surely Meg hadn't taken off without telling him? She couldn't be hiding from *him*? He was shocked by the sudden slam of panic that clutched at his chest and stomach. Her terse note had piqued his ego, but now he was worried. Really worried.

He dialled Dolly Kirby's number. As soon as the opening pleasantries were over, he demanded, 'What's happened to Meg?'

'Oh, Sam.' There was an awkward pause. 'Meg's all right.' But Dolly's voice was decidedly cautious.

'You're sure about that?'

'Absolutely.'

'Quite certain, Dolly?'

'Yes,' she replied with an impatient huff. 'She telephoned me only yesterday.'

He let out a huge sigh of relief. He'd been so worried that something had happened to her. 'Where is she?'

'I'm afraid I can't tell you that.'

Something like a strangled gasp emerged from Sam's throat. 'You mean she asked you not to tell me?'

'For the time being.' Dolly's voice held none of its usual warmth and Sam's chest tightened painfully. What in the blazes was going on?

Meg couldn't do this.

'Do you know why she's—avoiding me?'

'I just know she doesn't want you in her life.'

'Dolly!' Sam was embarrassed by the angry hurt that sounded so clearly in his voice, but he couldn't help shouting, 'This is ridiculous!'

'Sam, from what I hear you have plenty of girlfriends. Give Meg a break.'

'Girlfriends? I—I—That's in the past, Dolly.'

This comment was met by a threatening silence.

'Dolly? Don't you believe me?'

'I suspect there's more chance pigs will start flying,' Dolly responded dryly. 'Look, I'm sure Meg will contact you in her own good time.'

Knowing that was all he would get out of Dolly, Sam ended the conversation.

Dropping the receiver, he crossed his office floor and leaned his heated forehead against the cool plate-glass window. He stared at the tiny figures on the street below as they scurried about their business. What a mess!

He should never have left Australia without resolving the tensions between himself and Meg. It was obvious they'd got their wires crossed, but if he'd stayed another few days, he might have cleared the air.

It hit him like the proverbial brick, that he'd never met a woman like Meg. It wasn't just her loveliness, it was everything about her. The sound of her laughter. Her love for the sea and its creatures. He'd never known another woman whose interests so aligned with his—or what his would be if he were free to explore them.

Then there was that very special light in her eyes…her

natural elegance, the way she moved like a dancer...and her way of listening to him...and the way she made love...with such tenderness and passion...unrestrained sweetness and fire.

He wasn't quite sure what he wanted from her, but he was damned sure it was a hell of a lot more than a polite little rejection note. He'd give her a little while to calm down and then he'd try again. And as soon as he could settle his business matters, he would be searching for her. He wouldn't stop until he found her.

When Meg rang Dolly towards the middle of September, she was surprised to hear that Sam had tried several times to trace her.

'What did you tell him?'

'I—I tried to convince him that I didn't know where you were.'

'Did he believe you?'

'I'm not sure, but I didn't give anything away. I just told him you were heading south.'

'I bet that didn't satisfy him.'

Dolly laughed. 'It did not.' She mimicked Sam's angry response. *'South? How far south? There's an awful lot of Australia south of Townsville.'*

Meg clutched the phone to her chest. Talking about Sam always made her edgy. 'Do you think he's going to come looking for me?'

'I'm sure he will eventually, but at the moment he seems to be very caught up with his business.'

Meg bit back a retort. Of course he would be. Business and money. They were always number one with Sam.

Dolly's voice brightened. 'I told him you're keeping very well.'

'Dolly!' Meg cried. 'Why on earth did you say that? You'll make him suspect something.'

'No, dear. Men are thick about things like that. He just scoffed, "Of course she's well. Meg's a healthy young woman. Why shouldn't she be well?" And then I had to mumble something about flu.'

'I'm fighting fit,' Meg agreed. 'Just about over the early-morning blues.'

'That's wonderful, dear. Did you know Sam arranged for a team of nice men to paint my house for me? It looks beautiful now.'

'It's the least he could do, Dolly.'

'And the man he hired to do my garden every week is wonderful. As for that beautiful pearl brooch on my birthday... Meg, Sam's a wonderful young man.'

'I'm sure half the women in Seattle would agree with you, but he can stay wonderful on the other side of the Pacific.'

'You don't mean that, dear.'

Meg didn't want to end up in another argument with Dolly about the wisdom of her actions. Dolly's reasoning was based on the assumption that Sam was as in love and as committed as her Tom had been and Meg didn't have the heart to set her straight.

'I'll warn you now that I'm sure he will come looking for you just as soon as he's settled his business matters,' Dolly assured Meg.

Just how much time it would take to settle business matters surprised even Sam. It wasn't just a case of organising a satisfactory settlement with Dolly. Sam had other plans for the company. He wanted to sell it.

Getting his father's support had been the surprisingly easy part.

'Look what Kirby & Son has done to me,' the older man had sighed. 'Years and years of hard work and stress. My heart's so clapped out, I have to sit around like an invalid…taking things quietly…'

What took an infuriatingly long time was working his way through the minefield of negotiations involved in finding the right buyer. But the waiting and the patience were worth it. By Christmas, the last negotiations had taken place and by New Year a deal was finalised. The new owners were ecstatic and Sam's parents were happy.

And he felt like a man who'd been let out of jail.

Not a day had passed that he hadn't thought of Meg.

The day after the sale had gone through, he rang Dolly again.

There was a longish pause. 'I can't, Sam. I can't tell you where she is. I promised.'

'Not even a hint?'

'Why do you want to find her so badly?'

'You know why, Dolly. It's nearly eight months since I've seen her. And—damn it—I think I might be—in love with her.'

'You want to marry her?'

Sam gulped. 'I don't know—' He gulped again. 'Maybe.'

'Oh, dear,' the old lady whispered.

'Dolly.' Sam persisted. 'Think of Tom. I'm in the same situation Tom was. I travelled over to Australia and found this wonderful woman…'

'Yes. I know, dear.'

'So you're going to at least tell me which state she's in, aren't you?'

'Yes,' Dolly repeated more definitely. 'I think I shall.' She paused again while Sam's heart pounded. 'She's somewhere on the Sunshine Coast. In the beach house her father left her. But that's all I'm going to tell you. That's all I can say.'

'Dolly, you're an angel.'

But finding Meg was not going to be easy. The Sunshine Coast, Sam discovered when he arrived two days later, was a beautiful but heavily populated string of beaches north of Brisbane. There was Sunshine Beach, Coloundra, Noosa, Mooloolaba, Alexandra Headlands…an endless list.

He began his search in the telephone directory, working his way wearily through the Bennets. He hadn't realised it was such a common name. Finally, he decided that Meg must have an unlisted number.

Over the next few days, he walked the esplanades of a dozen beaches, scanning the crowds. And at least a dozen times he thought he saw her. Once in a car when he was crossing the road; he was almost run over when he stopped to stare at a woman with Meg's colouring. Another time he actually went up to a blonde woman in a coffee shop and tapped her on the shoulder but, when she turned around, she wasn't Meg.

He caught a glimpse of a woman at the far end of a shopping mall and was convinced she was Meg. But she was too far away and kept walking quickly with her back to him. With so many busy shoppers getting in his way, he continually bumped into people and kept having to stop to apologise. He couldn't catch a proper look at her.

And then, finally, she turned slightly and, silhouetted at the mall exit, he caught sight of a heavily pregnant stomach.

Another mistake. He knew then that it couldn't be Meg and he gave up the chase.

He tried ringing a few of the resorts in the area to see

if they employed a Meg Bennet but, as he expected, they didn't give out that kind of information.

Now, as he stopped for a snack at an outdoor cafe, he had to admit that his options were dwindling to nil. Defeat stared him in the face. He could consider a private detective. But if Meg didn't want to be found, what the hell was he doing searching for her? Maybe he should just give up. Get on with his life.

Most men in their early thirties would give an arm and a leg to be in his shoes—masses of money in the bank and no responsibilities. There was a whole world out there, and it was filled to overflowing with pretty women.

Why had he become fixated with just one?

One stubborn, mule-headed, obstinate woman, who didn't want him.

One beautiful, loving, passionate woman who, once upon a time, had wanted him with burning, breathless abandon.

He reached for his mobile phone. 'This is not a good afternoon, Dolly.'

'Sam, is that you? Have you found her?'

He released a rueful chuckle. 'You know you sent me on a wild-goose chase.'

'Oh, so you've had no luck?'

'Dolly, you've heard the cliché about needles and haystacks?'

'It's that bad?'

'Worse.' Sam rested an elbow on the table and propped his forehead with a clenched fist. He spoke slowly and firmly into the phone. 'I need her address. I'm worried about her. I *have* to find her.'

'Oh, Sam.' Dolly sighed. 'I think maybe you do. I hope I'm doing the right thing. Do you have a pen handy?'

She gave him an address.

And half an hour later he found Meg's house.

She wasn't home when he arrived, but he snooped in her letterbox and found mail addressed to her, so he knew at last he'd found her.

Hungry for details, Sam wandered around the yard of the small, rather shabby, beach cottage. Despite its lack of paint and the fact that the garden was no more than a stretch of grass and a few shady trees, it had a dilapidated charm.

At the back, a low porch looked out across the Maroochy River. Sam stepped onto it and a floorboard creaked beneath his weight. There were a couple of old cane chairs lined with faded patchwork cushions. A collection of potted herbs caught the afternoon sun in one corner, and from the edge of the roof dangled a mobile made from pieces of beach debris—driftwood, shells, fishing line and pieces of coral. It danced in the breeze and the shells tinkled softly.

An empty glass and a women's magazine had been left on the floor beside one of the chairs. There was a fishing rod propped in one corner. A faint aroma of bait clung to it. Beyond the porch, the wide river looked slow, like an old man enjoying the sun.

Sam lowered himself into one of the chairs and settled to wait, suddenly nervous. He was more than nervous, he was terrified. He'd been so focused on finding Meg that he hadn't planned the next step. And he needed to plan. He needed to get this absolutely right. So much was at stake.

One thing he knew. She wouldn't be welcoming him with wide open arms. A woman didn't go into hiding just for the sake of it. He hadn't a clue what her problem was. No one would give him answers.

He stared at the sleepy river and tried to think straight.

Negotiating a complicated business deal was child's play compared with handling Meg Bennet. Meg, with eyes that changed from grey to blue, or green, just as the sea did. Meg, with as many moods as the sea.

He stretched out his long legs and tried to relax. Surely it was just a simple misunderstanding. Once he saw her again, he would find a way to sort out their problem.

CHAPTER EIGHT

MEG was smiling as she left the hospital. The midwife had told her that her baby was growing really well— exactly the right size for her dates. The heartbeat was strong and Meg was fit as a fiddle. Everything was as it should be. She was on top of the world.

She'd been astounded at the way her thinking had changed in the past months. Pregnancy involved so much more than a drastic expansion of her waistline. Her baby had become the centre of her world. While people all around her carried on as usual, discussing politics, the nation's economy or global warming, Meg found her vision growing more and more inward.

For her, the only significant event of the year was the birth of her child.

As the baby grew, she loved it more fiercely every day. Once in a while she got depressed when she thought about the responsibilities that faced her alone in the future.

But at least she was over Sam.

Moving away from the island had been the best thing she'd ever done. She'd been able to start afresh on her own. Her baby was the love of her life these days and, after the midwife's glowing report today, she knew she had absolutely nothing to worry about.

When she turned into her street and saw a sleek blue sports car parked outside her house, she felt a stab of dismay. She had no idea who it could be, so when she turned onto the dirt car track at the side of the house, she edged her car forward very cautiously.

There was a figure, waiting on the back porch.

Her heart began to thump so loudly she feared for her health.

It couldn't be. It couldn't possibly be…

Sam!

White-knuckled, her hands gripped the steering wheel. She stared back at him through the rear window and her heart drummed a desperate tattoo. Sam was lounging against the timber railing. Dressed in faded jeans and an even more faded black T-shirt, he looked completely at home. And as sexy as ever. Oh, sweet heaven, what was she going to do?

He couldn't come back into her life now.

Not now.

Breathless and panicky, she tried to think straight. How on earth had he found her? Thoughts of backing down the drive and taking off flashed through her mind.

But he was already coming down the steps.

Her shaking fingers fumbled with the ignition key.

He crossed the grass towards her and stopped a few feet from the car. She could see his smile through the passenger window.

'Hi there.'

How could she stay? She didn't have the courage to face him when he discovered about the baby. In sheer panic, Meg wrenched the key forward and the engine flared to life. Stepping on the accelerator, she began to back down the drive.

She heard Sam's shout and the car stalled.

She knew she was being irrational. Struggling to think calmly, she told herself that trying to run was ridiculous. Anyway, there was no place she could go. He would follow her, or he would wait until she came back. She couldn't stay away forever.

And, as if he had known that she couldn't escape, Sam stood waiting, his expression an unreadable mask, while she inched the car forward again.

'Hello,' she called and her heart continued its painful thump, thump, thumping.

He ducked his head to look at her through the passenger window. 'Good to see you at long last.'

She nodded.

'How are you?' His voice quaked a little, showing her he was probably as nervous as she was. He looked paler than she remembered, but his eyes were the same mesmerising, slumberous blue. One look into them and she felt a familiar tug of longing.

'I—I'm fine,' she managed to reply. 'And you?'

'Just great.' His attempt at a grin fell short of the mark. 'Hey, are you going to get out of this car?'

No! she wanted to scream. Not till next Christmas. He still hadn't noticed she was the size of a whale. There was still a chance to escape.

In her dreams!

Reaching over, she picked up her purse and two grocery bags from the passenger seat, shoved her squeaky door open, and stood with her packages hiding her stomach. From her side of the car, she looked at him over its bonnet.

He looked back at her and the intensity of his gaze showed her that this wasn't just a casual, passing visit. 'Anything else you need out of the boot?' he said volunteering.

She shook her head.

Get moving, she silently ordered her feet and at last she began a slow journey around the front of her car, avoiding meeting his eyes. She didn't want to see his face when he first recognised her condition.

But when she reached Sam and he didn't speak for the longest time, she was forced to look up.

And she knew as soon as she did that, to the end of her days, she would never forget the expression on his face.

'*Meg!*'

His agonised cry cut straight to her heart.

'There's been a little change in my life,' she whispered with a self-conscious dip of her head.

Pale-faced, he stared at her pregnant stomach, shaking his head slowly and obviously unable to speak.

So many times she'd pictured a scene like this because, somehow, she'd known Sam would find her. She'd envisioned his anger, his surprise, even his elation. But her imagination had never pictured him looking so frighteningly shocked—as if she'd dropped from the clouds and crashed to the ground right in front of him.

In the face of such raw, unprotected emotion, her plans to be cool and distant vanished. 'Come inside,' she said gently, feeling close to tears. 'I'll make you a cuppa. Or maybe you need something stronger?'

With another dazed shake of his head, he followed her.

Inside, Meg kept herself from thinking and feeling by fussing about making tea and pouring a Scotch for Sam. She felt light-headed—as if this whole scene was some kind of hallucination. When she took a mug from the cupboard, she rubbed it against the palm of one hand, as if needing the reassurance of its everyday smooth coolness.

'How far—when?'

His voice coming from behind, startled her. She spun around. 'The baby's due in three weeks.'

She could see him trying to calculate dates and she offered him the Scotch, which he tossed down in one angry gulp.

'Does that mean—?' He set the empty glass on a nearby book shelf and, shoving both hands deep in his pockets, squared his jaw and nodded his head in the direction of her middle. 'Am I the—?' He swallowed and tried again. 'Is it mine?'

Now it was Meg's turn to be shocked. 'How could you ask such a thing? Of course it's yours—I mean, of course you're the father.'

'But I don't see how. I used protection.'

'I know we did. They don't always work, but that's not your fault. I knew a baby was the last thing you'd want.'

She turned quickly back to the business of making tea. 'Find a seat.' She tossed the instruction quickly over her shoulder. 'I'll join you in a minute.'

It was a sign of how shocked he was, she decided, that, like an obedient child, he returned to the back porch and sat staring out at the river.

A baby!

Sam dropped his head into his hands while his stomach heaved. His emotions were rioting. In all the months he'd been worrying about Meg, knowing that she'd taken off, he'd never thought of this little bombshell. A baby! *His child!* He was damned if he knew how the pregnancy had happened. He'd been careful!

But what about Meg? Here he was feeling sorry for himself, but what a time she must have had. And what a blow to the old ego that she wanted to keep this to herself. She hadn't been able to trust him to be there for her.

Lifting his head, he stared out at the river. It was so

peaceful and languid in contrast to the turmoil raging inside him. *How could she read him so wrong?*

He felt hot prickles behind his eyelids and swiped at his eyes with a hasty action he hoped she didn't see.

Meg's hands shook as she brought the mugs outside. For an uncomfortable stretch of time, they sat side by side staring at the river without speaking.

'Now I know why Dolly made such a big deal about how well you're keeping,' Sam said at last.

'Dolly's been wonderful,' Meg admitted. 'I wanted her to know because, in a way, she's the baby's great grandmother.'

'Oh, yeah,' Sam snapped bitterly. 'Tell the step-great-grandmother, but not the father. That's really neat thinking.'

Meg felt her cheeks flame. 'I tried to ring you as soon as I found out. But I got one of your snooty girlfriends on your line.'

Sam frowned as he thought for a moment. 'I think that must have been Julia.' He let out a long, bitter sigh. 'She wasn't a girlfriend.'

'Whatever,' Meg responded. Who was he trying to kid? 'But even if I hadn't spoken to her, I still knew it was in my best interests to forget about you, Sam.'

'Why?' he yelled. An angry flush reddened his face.

'Please,' she whispered. 'Let's not fight about this.'

He sighed again. 'Just give me a little moment or two to—to adjust. I'm sure I'll behave myself when I get a little more used to the idea.'

She wriggled in her seat to get more comfortable. Her baby's foot was kicking hard against her ribs. Suddenly, she felt cold as if a rogue breeze had crept across the river. She sipped at her rose-hip tea. There was no way to make this easy.

Sam wasn't going to just wish her well and saunter off into the sunset like a vagabond cowboy. This was going to be the awful part, when he started to get possessive.

As if on cue, he took a deep swig from the mug and then turned to her hastily. 'I'm quite willing to marry you.'

Her eyes widened with shock.

'Sorry if that was too blunt,' he muttered. 'It didn't come out quite the way I meant it.'

'I certainly don't expect you to marry me, Sam. In fact, it's the *last* thing I expect—or want.'

'Last thing, eh? That's what I thought.' He looked away again.

'I've never believed in people marrying just because there's a baby on the way.'

'I can always help with finances, of course.'

'Sam,' she said, and her voice cracked on the single syllable, 'you don't have to worry about me. I'm managing just fine. I mean that.'

'What about after the baby's born? How will you manage then?'

'I have some money. And I'll study. Eventually, I'll go back into marine science.'

'What about the baby?'

'What about it?'

'Are you keeping it?'

'Of course. And don't you even think of lining up those lawyers of yours for some kind of paternal rights contract.'

He frowned. 'So you're quite settled on bringing up a little kid all on your own?'

'Yes.' She wished her answer sounded more definite. She meant it to sound totally convincing.

His face grew tight. 'Or do you have some other guy lined up for the job? A new daddy for little…'

'Of course there's no one else.' Jumping up, she stomped across the porch to stand near the railing with her back to him, hiding her quivering chin. When her anger had dropped from boiling to simmering, she turned back to him. 'For Pete's sake, Sam. That's twice already you've suggested I might have another man hidden away somewhere. Another lover. That's your department. It's not my style at all.'

'I just want to understand your situation,' he muttered defensively.

Meg took a huge breath. 'OK. Here's the situation It's quite simple really.' She held up one hand and, with the other, she ticked off her fingers as she made each point. 'We had a brief relationship. We made love once. You went home again, back to being Seattle's favourite bachelor. Now I'm pregnant. And I'm dealing with it. This baby's mine.'

'And mine. And normally—'

'Please,' she hissed through gritted teeth, clutching the mug tightly against her. 'I agree that, as the father, you have some rights, but don't start talking about *normally*. We don't have a normal situation. We both agreed when you left the island that marriage isn't part of our game plan.'

He rose and closed the gap between them. Meg shut her eyes. Whenever he came close, some traitorous part of her brain began to think about being closer. And that was insane.

'I can see where you're coming from,' he said with a

heavy sigh. 'When I left last year, there was too much still up in the air.'

She turned to the river and opened her eyes to stare out across the stretch of water.

'And, now, I guess it's too late,' Sam added.

'Yes!' Meg almost spat out the word. Then, ridiculously, she shot him a suspicious glance. 'Too late for what?'

He stood beside her, looking, as she was, at the river. 'Too late to start at the beginning and get things right.'

She nodded.

'If we had gone about this by the usual route,' he suggested slowly, 'we would have got to know each other over time—then we might have married—and *then* had kids. Things might have worked out. Might have even been perfect.'

'Please don't go on,' Meg implored him. 'There's no point in going over how things might have been.'

He persisted, in spite of her protest. 'But you're right. We met for a few days. There was a spark—'

'A spark?' she echoed, sounding surprisingly hurt even to her own ears. 'Is that what happened?'

His eyes held hers and, for the first time that afternoon, she saw a glimmer of the old humour she'd learned to expect from Sam. 'Actually,' he said with a slow grin that sent uncalled for waves of longing rippling through her, 'it was more like spontaneous combustion, wasn't it?'

She refused to answer, but suspected that her flaming cheeks did the job for her.

'And, hey presto!' He gestured towards her bulging middle. 'We skipped a whole bunch of vital steps in between.'

Meg's chin lifted. 'I don't think that means we should

automatically try to fill in the gaps now. You can't do relationships dot-to-dot.'

'No.' He sighed.

She crossed her arms over her chest, hugging herself. 'And that is exactly why I gave up trying to contact you.'

'But you can't keep me out of this, Meg,' he said softly.

She refused to answer.

'I'm already a part of it.'

Her chin lifted defiantly.

He went on. 'This little kid is half mine. As much as you might be trying to overlook the fact, you can't ignore the genetics. Your baby will be wearing my genes.'

She flashed a heated glance in his direction. 'But that doesn't give you the right to intrude into my life. I need you to respect my privacy.'

'You've had eight months of privacy.'

'Sam...' her voice held a note of warning '...I've spent that time adjusting. And I've done well. I've got it all together now. Leave me alone. You—you've done the wrong thing tracking me down.'

It was his turn to be silent. He stood staring into the distance and he tapped at her driftwood mobile with one lean finger, setting it swaying so that the shells clinked against each other.

Meg watched, feeling wretched.

Finally, he turned her way. 'We've probably said enough for the moment. We're both upset and we need a little space to—adjust.'

She nodded.

He crossed to the top of the porch steps and Meg wondered why she didn't feel relieved that he was leaving so soon.

'You're staying somewhere on the coast?' she asked.

He nodded, but she noticed he didn't seem to want to give her any details. 'I guess you should get some rest, Meg, and drink plenty of milk, or whatever it is that's good for pregnant women. I'll be in touch.'

Grabbing the rail, he swung himself down the low steps in one bound and jogged back down the car tracks as if he couldn't get away from her fast enough.

Sam resisted the urge to ring Meg or visit her the next day. And the next. Instead he visited the local library and unearthed a stack of books. She wanted her space and, for his part, he had a lot to learn.

Aside from how they started, he knew nothing about babies. He'd never given any considered thought to anything remotely linked to babies. Had never touched one— not even tentatively on the toe. The whole concept of fatherhood wasn't one he'd ever applied to himself.

Now, late in the afternoon, he was grappling with a staggering information overload.

He phoned her.

'Meg speaking,' she answered, sounding relaxed...and beautiful.

'It's me,' Sam announced. 'How are you?'

'Fine thanks.'

Had he imagined it, or was there a tinge of warmth in her answer? 'Doing anything exciting?'

'Oh, yes. My life is a thrill a minute. At the moment I'm ironing a maternity smock.'

A sudden picture of a domesticated, rosy-cheeked Meg, pregnant and standing at an ironing board, danced into his mind. Why the image should seem incredibly sexy was beyond him. It must be what happened to a guy after long periods of abstinence.

He banged a hand against his forehead in an effort to

clean up his thoughts. 'I was wondering if you've developed any of those food cravings that pregnant women get?'

'Curried spaghetti,' she responded impulsively.

He chuckled. 'That's an original one. Do you make it from your own recipe?'

'I like the tinned version best.'

'Uh-huh.' He paused for a moment. 'Anything else?'

'Hot chocolate with marshmallows. Sam, why do you want to know?'

'Just curious. I can see you've developed quite a sophisticated palate.'

'Most of the time I eat a well-balanced diet.'

'Glad to hear it.' He muttered as he scribbled a few notes. 'OK. I can do that.'

'Do what? What are you talking about?'

'I'm bringing dinner. My shout. I'll be there around six-thirty.'

'But, Sam, there's no need.'

He didn't bother to argue, deciding it was safer just to hang up.

As she set the table with simple red and white striped table mats and crisply ironed white serviettes, Meg tried to tell herself that she wasn't at all pleased that Sam was visiting again and bringing dinner after staying away for two whole days. Two tension-packed days when she'd wondered what on earth he was doing.

She ought to be dampening her unsuitable enthusiasm by focusing on the last time Sam offered to fix a meal for her. The exotic seafood dinner that had never happened. That had been the worst night of her life.

She also had to apply her thoughts to how to get rid of him quickly. He hadn't given her time to explain that she had a childbirth education class to attend this evening.

There was a knock at her front door and she hurried to open it.

Sam smiled down at her as he entered her hallway, carrying a shopping bag. His big frame was silhouetted against the setting sun and he looked like heaven in blue jeans. Her breath caught and her silly heart trembled with delight.

She'd been too distraught the other day, to dwell on his good looks but, tonight, she couldn't help registering every ruggedly masculine detail.

He dropped a kiss on her cheek so quickly, she didn't have time to duck. 'I didn't tell you the other day how lovely you look,' he said. 'Motherhood really suits you, Nutmeg.'

The unexpected compliment and the old nickname caught her unprepared. She couldn't hold back a pleased smile.

In her kitchen, he unloaded a bag of groceries and set them out on the bench. 'I could only find little tins of curried spaghetti.'

Smiling self-consciously, she nodded. 'I doubt it's the most popular item on the supermarket shelves.'

Besides the spaghetti tins, he'd brought a huge packet of fluffy pink marshmallows, a bag of green salad, some cherry tomatoes, a bottle of dressing and a litre of milk.

He grinned at her. 'A simple but tasty menu. How do you like your curried spaghetti?'

'Heated on toast.'

'Might I suggest a side salad?'

'That would be lovely, Sam.' Meg lifted a hasty hand to her mouth as she listened to herself. *That would be lovely, Sam.* What kind of limp-willed Lizzie was she? It was happening again. He was slapping on the charm. She was letting down her guard. The next thing she knew they'd be...

She shook her head. Next thing, if she had her way, he would be heading back to Seattle. After many ambivalent months, when she'd been uncertain about her future, the recent weeks had brought a reassuring feeling of focus and balance.

She knew what she wanted now: a simple, quiet life for her and her baby. She certainly didn't want a playboy millionaire pulling her strings as if she was a mindless puppet.

'How's your business?' she asked and was surprised when he didn't answer for quite some moments. She didn't think the long pause was justified by the difficulty of opening a tin of spaghetti.

'The business is fine,' he said at last. 'I've left it in good hands.'

'Your parents?'

'They're well. At least Dad's as well as can be expected. Where do you keep your microwave cooking gear?'

She showed him and, while he attended to the spaghetti, Meg made toast.

'I've been reading about ultrasound,' Sam said casually. 'Have you had that?'

'Yes.'

'And?'

'It showed that the baby's fine. Everything is as it should be.'

'That's great.' He adjusted the timer on the microwave and straightened to look down at her searchingly. 'So did they tell you the baby's sex?'

She nodded.

'Will you tell me?'

Meg drew in a sharp breath, remembering how real the baby had become for her once she'd known its gender. That kind of insider knowledge would bring Sam another step closer. Telling him probably wasn't wise.

'I'm just asking out of idle curiosity,' he added, almost too offhandedly.

She gave in. Keeping the news to herself had been hard. 'It's a boy.' She nibbled her upper lip.

His blue eyes—the eyes she so hoped her baby had inherited—widened. Then his face broke into an incredulous smile. 'A boy? That's kind of amazing isn't it?'

'You have a preference for boys?'

'Me? Not especially. I love girls.'

'Of course you do,' Meg muttered under her breath.

'I'm sure girl babies are especially cute. It's just…now I know it's a boy. Heck, it just brings home that your bump—' he indicated to her stomach with a nod of his head '—is aging to be a real, living, breathing person.'

'It hits you all of a sudden,' she agreed.

He returned to slicing tomatoes, but then he shot another cheeky grin in her direction. 'Hey, he'll need someone to teach him how to pitch a baseball.'

Startled, Meg cried, 'Hang on, Sam, don't get carried away. To start with, you won't be here. Secondly, this baby's going to be an Australian. He won't be playing baseball. He'll be learning to surf and playing cricket. He'll be—'

He held up his hands to slow her down. 'My apologies. I get the picture.' He surveyed the kitchen. 'Anyway, before we get too het up about our kid's future, I think this simple banquet is ready.'

With some misgivings about the way this evening was heading, Meg handed him two plates and he dished up their spaghetti on toast as carefully as he might a gourmet meal. And, as they carried their plates and glasses of milk through to her little dining room, he added, 'Do you have a video of the ultrasound?'

She only just restrained a sigh. 'I do.'

They sat down to eat before he said, 'I'd really like to take a look at it later.'

'I may not have time this evening. I have—an appointment.' She began to give her food her serious attention. For a few moments they ate in silence.

'What's it like?' he asked suddenly. 'Being pregnant?'

She couldn't help smiling. 'Fantastic.'

Both his eyebrows rose. 'So you don't feel trapped, betrayed by your biology…any of those feminist urges?'

'I did at first.'

He frowned.

'For about five minutes.'

'I wish I'd known. I would have been here earlier.'

'The first few months weren't worth watching. I hung over a bucket for ages. But the rest has been fine.'

'Do you know much about looking after babies?'

Was this a trap? Some kind of test? Meg considered pretending she was a baby-care expert, but her natural honesty prevailed. 'Not a lot,' she admitted. 'But I've bought heaps of books.' Looking down at her plate, she added, 'I don't seem to be able to think much past the birth at the moment.'

His eyes grew serious as he looked at her. 'I can never get my head around that whole delivery bit. Scares me witless just to think about it.' Then he looked embarrassed. 'I guess that doesn't make you feel any better.'

'I'm sure I'll be OK,' she said with forced cheerfulness. 'After all, look how many women have babies every day.'

She realised that she was starting to let down her guard. Here she was chatting away to Sam as if he was— a close friend. Continued loneliness could have that effect—of grasping at straws.

He frowned. 'But you're planning on doing all this on you own?'

'Yes,' she admitted unwillingly. 'Of course, there's a midwife…'

Sam shoved his plate aside, rested his elbows on the table and propped his chin in his hands. 'Meg, I think you're being selfish about this.'

'Selfish?' she cried. *'Selfish?'* How dared he make such a claim! Did he have any idea how much she'd given up?

Obviously he didn't. He continued his lecture. 'Look at your situation.'

'I *am* looking at it from the inside—day in, day out.' Her voice rose several decibels. 'This baby and I have been superglued to each other for some time now.'

'Sure,' he agreed with infuriating calm. 'But how about you listen to another point of view? '

She opened her mouth to protest. And shut it. 'OK, Mr Wise Guy,' she retorted shakily. 'You explain to me exactly what I'm doing that's so wrong.'

'Well, you've come down here, isolating yourself from your friends and your support base.' He paused. 'That's right, isn't it? You don't have family. Do you have friends here on the coast who know you well and are willing to be there for you?'

'I'm doing fine.'

'But you're going it *alone,* Meg.'

'That's the way I like it.'

He shook his head. 'Hell, it's not what being a human being is about. You wouldn't be clinging so stubbornly to this independence thing if you really thought about what's best for the baby.'

'How dare you!' she cried. Her knife and fork clattered to her plate as she glared at him.

Not the slightest bit intimidated by her anger, Sam reached across the table and touched his knuckles to her cheek—a gentle, feather-soft caress. Her heart jumped crazily.

'I dare because I—' his throat seemed to stick on whatever he'd planned to say '—I think someone should keep an eye on you.'

'I keep telling you, I'm fine.'

He shook his head. 'You might be fine but, whether you like it or not, I'm going to stick around till the baby's born.'

The cheek of him! Meg spluttered, overcome by the nerve of this man handing down his edict. She'd been managing on her own for so long... 'You want to swan around here and then as soon as the hard work's done you'll come bouncing into the hospital ward handing out cigars and announcing, ''He's mine''?'

She knew she sounded catty, but she couldn't help it.

He surprised her by answering quietly, 'That's not what I'm on about at all. If you want me to, I'll leave as soon as I know you and the baby are fine. But, in the meantime, count me in.'

He looked so determined, like a fiercely beautiful guardian angel, she could feel all her arguments snapping, as if the strings that held them together had been cut with a single slash of a knife.

'You mean it? Once the baby's born, you won't start making demands? You won't be wanting to turn him into Samuel Kirby II or something? '

'Of course I mean it.'

'You promise you'll leave once the baby's born?'

He stared straight back at her, his eyes unflinching. 'I'll go, if that's what you want.'

'You're not going to try to—resume our relationship?'

He looked away and she saw the muscles in his neck grow tense but, when his eyes returned to lock with hers, he said, 'If you're not interested, what's the point?'

She sucked in her breath. 'No point at all. So, you're prepared to—'

'I want to support you through these last few weeks. My hotel is only twenty minutes away from here. I can drive you to the hospital in the middle of the night. The things prospective fathers usually do.' He took a small notebook out of his back pocket and scribbled on a page, tore it out and handed it to her. 'That's my mobile number and my address. Any time you're worried about anything, call me.'

It was a seductive idea. Meg hadn't admitted it to anyone but, as her time grew nearer, her courage had encountered one or two stumbling blocks.

She sent him a challenge. 'If you really want to help, prove it.'

'I'd be happy to, but how?'

'Come to my childbirth education class with me this evening.'

For a second or two she thought she'd caught him out. His eyes widened. His Adam's apple moved up and down. 'Fathers go to those things, do they?'

'Sure.'

'And it's just a class? We'll just sit around and take instruction, won't we?'

'There's a little more to it than that,' she mumbled. In fact, she was rapidly questioning her sanity. Why on earth had she thrown out that invitation? It was a crazy idea. All the other couples were married or in committed relationships.

Frantically, she juggled words in her heard, trying to figure the best way to retract her challenge.

But it was too late. Sam was already smiling and saying, 'I'd be happy to come.'

CHAPTER NINE

FOLLOWING Meg's directions, Sam drove her to the class. He pulled up the hood of his convertible and drove extra carefully, aware of his precious cargo. Tense and silent, Meg sat beside him, looking adorable in a black stretch-knit tunic and tights. Her hair was arranged into a cute little knot of wheat-coloured curls on top of her head.

He kept wanting to look at her. He'd never noticed before how attractive a pregnant woman could be. Until three days ago, he'd found them about as sexy as rolled oats.

The classes were held in a low building at the back of the hospital and, as they stepped into the room, he was unprepared for the enthusiastic greetings of the other couples.

A pale redhead with a stomach as round as two water-melons and with a square-jawed husband in tow, rushed forward screeching, 'Meg!' She dropped her voice to a stage whisper, 'Is this *him*? Your baby's father?'

Meg nodded shyly.

'Way to go!' The woman laughed. She grabbed Sam's hand. 'It's great to see you here—um—'

'Sam,' he supplied.

'This is Carol,' Meg explained quickly. 'And Todd.'

'Hey, where're you from, Sam?'

'Seattle.'

Carol beamed at him as if he were some kind of su-perstar. She winked at Meg. 'I can see why you've been hiding him, honey.'

Others gathered close and Carol took on the job of introducing Sam as if he were a special discovery. Everyone's excitement for Meg now that her baby's father had shown up was downright embarrassing. Sam was relieved when someone announced that a girl called Sara had given birth to a baby girl that morning and attention was suddenly directed away from him.

Excited cries and a hundred questions filled the next few minutes, but the arrival of a middle-aged woman with iron-grey hair brought the discussion to a halt. The couples took their places on yoga-style mats on the floor.

'Is everybody ready to talk about second-stage labour tonight?' the woman asked with a hearty chuckle. 'When we get to that point, we know the job's almost done.'

She paused and her eyes rounded as she saw Sam. He'd been trying to look unobtrusive as he sat on the floor beside Meg with his elbows resting nonchalantly on his bent knees.

She beamed at Meg and gave a little approving nod of her head. 'We have a newcomer in our class?'

Shyly, Meg made another introduction.

'Great to have you on board, Sam. Are you going to attend Meg's confinement?'

'Attend?' He gulped. *Attend the birth? Hell, no.* 'I—I don't know. I'm just her back-up support. I get to drive the car and carry the bags.'

One of the fathers behind him chuckled. 'You were there at the start, mate. They'll make sure you're there at the end.'

The instructor smiled serenely. 'That's for Meg and Sam to decide.' She looked around the room. 'Before we discuss your baby's delivery, let's go over some of our relaxation breathing. Nice, deep, slow breaths, now, mothers. We're having minute long contractions. Fathers, you can breathe along with them. Cleansing breath, and…'

Sam found his eyes riveted on Meg as she breathed. She sat cross-legged on the floor, with her eyes closed, and he could feel her drawing inward, focusing on something only she could find.

After a few, deep slow breaths, her right hand came up and slowly, slowly, she began to massage her rounded tummy—in big, soft circles. He could see her body relaxing. Her shoulders began to slump and her jaw to sag a little more as each breath was released.

She looked beautiful.

To his amazement, she lifted the black top she was wearing and exposed her bare abdomen. All of a sudden, he felt as if he'd swallowed a block of wood—perhaps an entire tree stump. He could see the true shape of her. Her skin looked so soft and creamy—and a faint line had appeared exactly down her middle. Now, she was trailing her fingertips over her skin, massaging once more. His eyes followed her fingers and he imagined how she must feel—so soft and warm.

He remembered a time when her hands had caressed his body and a film of sweat broke out all over him.

'Fathers,' the teacher was saying, 'remember, you can help during the first stage of labour, by reminding your wife to relax like this—or by rubbing her back if she has backache.'

Sam hadn't touched Meg for so long, the thought of rubbing her back—any part of her—brought an uncalled for thrust of desire. He took a deep breath. Time to try some relaxing of his own.

'Just remember not to over-breathe so that you hyperventilate. OK, that's great. This last contraction is coming to an end.'

He watched as Meg's eyes opened slowly. She looked at him, blushed prettily and pulled her tunic top back over her stomach.

He leaned close. 'You were fantastic. The best breather in the whole class.'

Looking pleased but also self-conscious, she gave him a playful push.

'What we're going to talk about for the rest of tonight is usually the most exciting stage of labour,' their teacher went on. 'When you feel the urge to push, you know it won't be long before you see your baby. For the first delivery, pushing may take a few minutes or up to three hours.'

Three hours! Sam hoped his shock didn't show.

He listened, fascinated, as the instructor went on to describe the various positions a woman might like to consider when pushing out her baby—squatting, lying on her side, on her back. He tried to switch off his imagination when she began to talk about stretching, burning, stinging sensations but, for the most part, he found himself listening carefully. If he couldn't be there with Meg, at least he could understand what was going to happen.

'OK,' she said at last, sweeping aside some charts she'd used to illustrate the progress of a baby down the birth canal, 'that's enough theory for tonight. Let's do some practice. I want each couple to choose a birthing position.'

Meg turned to Sam. 'I'll try lying on my side,' she said.

He tried to answer, but his throat wouldn't make a sound, so he nodded.

She stretched out on the strip of foam rubber, obviously unaware of the way her graceful movements af-

fected him. It took all Sam's self-control not to get right
down beside her.

'I'm—er—I'm going to have to support your leg,' he
whispered.

She nodded and smiled, her silvery grey eyes glinting
with a touch of amusement.

Damn her! She was enjoying his discomfort.

He crawled on his knees till he was positioned at the
appropriate angle and then he touched her thigh. A quick
glance around the room showed him the other guys were
grabbing hold of different parts of their women without
turning a hair.

It was all right for them, he thought. They curled up
with their baby's mothers every night. They were kissing
them night, noon and morning.

But he hadn't touched Meg in eight months—and even
then it had never become a habit. Sweat beaded his brow.
This was the first time he'd touched her in all this time
and he was having to hold her legs apart. And on top of
that he was supposed to keep breathing!

Fate, he decided, had a strange sense of humour.

'Are all our little fathers in place?' the teacher called.

There was a smattering of replies. Sam muttered something rude beneath his breath.

'Right. We're getting the urge to push. Here it comes.
Tilt your pelvis, mothers. Round your shoulders, put your
chin on your chest—and—push! That's it. Push, again!
Keep pushing—a little more. That's it. Have a rest.' She
beamed at her class. 'Well done.'

Sam lowered Meg's leg.

She smiled up at him and he only just resisted the urge
to lean down and kiss her teasing lips. 'How are you
doing?' she asked.

He wiped a shaky hand over his damp brow and tried

to crack a grin. 'Piece of cake,' he told her. 'By the time your baby comes, we won't need a midwife.'

Half an hour later, he emerged from the class, feeling a little shell-shocked, but rather pleased with himself. 'I'm an educated man,' he said to Meg as he walked with her towards the car.

She smiled back at him. 'You had your mouth hanging open for most of the night—especially during the film. I almost leaned over and shut it for you.'

He sent her what he hoped was a smile. They had reached the car and they both stood beside her door. Sam, about to open it, paused. 'You shouldn't talk about mouths and touching in the same breath, Meg Bennet.'

In the glow of a street light, her eyes shimmered as she looked cautiously up at him. Her slightly parted lips looked rounded, soft and sweet.

He lowered his head.

'Sam,' Meg whispered, 'there are people around!'

Of course there were.

With his lips millimetres from hers, he paused, then lifted his head again. What was he thinking of? There were car doors opening and shutting all around them. A dozen pairs of curious eyes had swivelled in their direction. He contented himself with sliding his thumb softly across her lower lip. She was petal soft…and she didn't pull away.

'Is it pregnancy that makes you softer and lovelier than ever?' he asked.

He heard her surprised gasp. She looked as if she wanted to cry.

Hastily he dropped his hand and opened the passenger door for her. And, as he hurried around to the driver's side, he cursed himself for a fool. His brains had dropped below his belt. If there was any way he was going to work out where he and Meg were heading, it wasn't by trying to get her back into bed.

Meg spent the next twenty minutes giving herself a long, silent lecture while Sam drove through the quiet back streets towards her home. Heavens, she was a lustful beast. And a foolish one. Sam had only to drop one little compliment—one *tiny* compliment—and she was ready to hurl herself into his arms.

Hadn't she learned anything since last May? Listening to his appealing sweet-talk had got her into this mess in the first place.

If only she didn't feel so physically attracted to him. She had expected that being pregnant would provide her with a measure of protection from his sex appeal. But she'd only had to compare him with every other man she'd seen in the past few days to know that he was one in a million. And that he still had the power to make her want him.

She'd felt a curious pride in him tonight. A feeling, she realised now, that she wasn't in any way entitled to enjoy. Sam might be the baby's father, but he didn't belong to her. Nor she to him. They had made a mistake, but they'd both agreed that, once the baby was born, they had to get on with their separate lives.

They were a contemporary couple. They weren't victims of the old rules that insisted that a couple expecting a baby should marry.

She tried to picture their future.

Ten years from now, Sam would pop over from the States for their son's birthday. He would bring his charming American wife and their handsome, intelligent children. Meg would probably be married to someone else and she and her husband might have a child of their own. They would be the kind of patchwork family that existed quite happily all over the place these days. The various adults and children would all be thoroughly nice to each other.

Everyone would marvel at how well they all got on.

A new millennium family.

It was only when the lights of the houses they passed began to grow fuzzy that Meg realised she was crying. Surreptitiously, she blotted her tears with her sleeve. Why did such a practical and sensible, *realistic* picture of the future make her feel so sad?

She stole a sneak look at Sam. Illuminated by passing street lights, his profile wrenched her heart. Every little detail seemed utterly perfect—the jut of his nose, the sensual swell of his lips, the dark line of his jaw. Having him around—seeing him again—that was her problem. She'd never had an ounce of will-power where he was concerned.

Once this baby was born and he was gone, she would be able to get on with her life once more. She held on to that thought.

He brought the car to a stop outside her house and jumped out quickly, coming around to open her door. When he helped her out, she formed her lips to say the words good night. But she made the mistake of looking up.

And the look in his eyes stilled the words.

Meg's heart raced. He was standing close to her, their gazes locked. Under her ribs, her baby sent out a ferocious kick.

'What was that?' Sam stepped back a little.

'The baby.'

'Wow! The little guy kicks *that* hard?' He lifted his hand. 'Would you—would it be all right if I felt him?'

How could she refuse? Taking his hand in hers, she

placed it high on her stomach, exactly on the spot where the baby's foot always lay. Sensing the pressure, the little foot kicked again.

'Way to go, kid!' he exclaimed. 'That's a powerful kick. It's incredible.'

Meg's breath felt trapped in her throat. It felt ridiculously right to have his warm, strong hand there, under hers, cradling their baby.

His face was so close. Any minute, any *second* now, he might try to kiss her again. And if he didn't, she realised with a shock, she might go ahead and kiss him anyhow. Oh, how she wanted one or two of his kisses—his long and slow, sexy kisses right now. She'd been on her own for so long.

'Nutmeg,' he growled.

Strangely, it was the huskiness, the unmistakable shudder of desire in his voice that brought her to her senses, as sharply as a reprimand. The fact that he was wanting her as much as she longed for him, reminded her that this was a very dangerous game she was playing—getting close to Sam for just a little while.

She mustn't make the same mistake as last time.

Stepping quickly to one side, she drew away from him. Desperately, she struggled to think of something to say that had nothing to do with mouths or kissing. 'Would you like to see the ultrasound pictures of the baby?' she blurted out.

He stood, looking a little puzzled, his breathing a touch ragged. Sticking his thumbs into the loops of his jeans, he dropped his head to one side as he studied her carefully. 'Why not?' he asked at last. 'As long as it comes with a cup of hot chocolate and some marshmallows.'

Meg fumbled in her bag for her door key. 'Hot chocolate and a baby video,' she said with a shaky little laugh.

'What an exciting life Seattle's favourite bachelor leads these days.'

Seattle's favourite bachelor.

As he followed Meg into her house, the words echoed in Sam's head. If only she knew the half of it. The press's image of him as a playboy bachelor had died a quick and painless death in the past six months. Journalists had hovered around him for a few weeks after his return from Australia. When they discovered that he spent all his days and a hefty chunk of his nights closeted in his office, they pestered him for an explanation, but he sent them packing with a few cutting comments and they soon gave up.

He wondered how Meg would react if he told her the truth about his lack of social life since he'd seen her last. She probably wouldn't believe it.

It *was* rather unbelievable, he reflected now. If anyone asked him to explain why he'd given up dating other women since he returned to Seattle, he would be hard pressed to find a plausible answer. But the old appetite just wasn't there any more. A pretty woman was just that—a pretty woman. She wasn't—

'Here's the video,' Meg said, thrusting a slim rectangular box into his hand. 'You set it up, while I make the hot chocolate.' She hurried away into the kitchen, calling over her shoulder, 'But don't start without me. I'll need to explain it to you.'

He had everything ready when Meg reappeared carrying steaming mugs topped with fluffy pink marshmallows. They were almost overflowing. She set them down carefully on the coffee table beside some marine biology textbooks and then she fished two spoons out of her pocket.

'For scooping up the yummy bits,' she explained. She

took a seat on the sofa beside him. 'Can I have the remote? I'll need to stop and start so I can explain.'

'Sure.'

Sam dragged his gaze from the enticing vision of her flushed cheeks, dancing eyes and golden curls to the fuzzy black-and-white screen. At first, the video made no sense to him at all.

Meg pointed. 'Look, that little row of things like tiny rectangles shows the baby's spine. These are his fingers. Aren't they cute?' She gave a little giggle.

Fascinated, Sam hunched forward with his elbows resting on his knees. This was his son. A miraculous fusion of his and Meg's bodies.

'And there's his heart,' Meg was saying, her voice vibrating with hushed, happy warmth. 'You can see it beating.'

He located the tiny pulsating blob. 'It's so strong,' he whispered.

'It's beating at a hundred and thirty-six beats to the minute,' Meg elaborated, totally unaware of how radiant and utterly delicious she looked. 'Apparently that's a great speed for babies.'

'What about fathers?'

Her eyes shot to link with his. Her mouth rounded and stayed open as if she was going to ask a question, but changed her mind. She dampened her lower lip with her tongue.

Sam groaned.

'What about fathers, Sam?' she repeated his question.

'This one's heart has been galloping at a rate of knots all evening.'

'Oh.'

The urges that raged within him were frightening. He needed to pull Meg against him, to crush those soft pink lips against his and to plunder her beautiful, blossoming body. For most of the evening, he'd been envisaging a whole range of preposterous fantasies. All of them impossible.

And Meg wasn't helping things any. She was leaning towards him, looking flushed and making soft, breathy little sounds. Her eyes were grey pools with silver sparkles, like sunlight glinting off water.

If he didn't know better, he could swear she was inching closer, willing him to kiss her. But kissing Meg would be more temptation than he could handle right at this point in time. Like toppling dominoes, one thing would lead to another to…total disaster.

Meg was trusting him to keep his distance. He had promised her…

And he didn't know anything about making love to a pregnant woman. He was scared witless that he might actually hurt her if he stayed a minute longer. He jumped to his feet. 'That video was great…great to see the little guy. He looks in wonderful shape. But I'd better head off now. Let you get your beauty sleep.'

'What about your chocolate?'

'Oh, yeah. Thanks.' Scooping up the mug, he downed the drink in a long, scalding draught. Bits of marshmallow stuck to his lips and, chewing them off, he headed for the door.

'Thanks for coming to the class,' she called after him as he backed down her front steps.

'My pleasure,' he called back before vaulting her front gate and jogging to his car. Seconds later, he was accelerating down her street. In his rear-vision mirror he could see Meg standing in the yellow pool of light on her front porch, holding her front door open with one hand as she peered after him. The other hand was raised as if she'd been thinking about waving to him.

She looked so all alone.

He flicked his gaze back to the road and told himself that *alone* was exactly how Meg Bennet wanted to be.

With flaming cheeks, Meg watched the twin red tail lights disappear around the street corner. What on earth had come over her? She'd been cosying up to Sam on the sofa and had been seriously thinking about seducing him.

She'd wanted to get closer to the tantalising scent of him. She had visions of tracing her tongue over the dark shadow of his jaw, teasing him into kissing her. She had even imagined undoing the buttons of his denim shirt and sliding her hand over the hard planes of his chest.

Thank goodness her whale-like figure had put him off. The way he'd made a beeline for her front door had hardly been flattering, but at least it had saved her from making a foolish mistake.

If they had begun to kiss, or to do any of the dozen other things her febrile brain had been considering, all of her other carefully framed plans would have been ruined. She could hardly have her lustful way with Sam again and then insist on keeping him at arm's length for the rest of her life.

After standing, staring into the night for a long time, she wandered back into the house. Her cooled cup of chocolate was sitting on the coffee table. The pink marsh-mallows had melted and had begun to dissolve. They no longer looked tempting. The video had run through and her blank television screen cast a fuzzy light into the room.

Damn Sam! Up until now, she'd been managing so well on her own. She'd pushed him right to the back of her mind over the past months and she had become completely absorbed with her baby. She hadn't needed anyone else. All her emotions had been taken up by her growing son.

Almost every magazine she picked up these days carried a story about single mothers—fiercely independent women, loving their lives, free of the need to divide their loyalty between their baby and a man.

And now, here was Sam, back in her life, looking divine, charming her senseless, making her want him and totally messing her up again.

Switching off the television, she gathered up the mugs and carried them through to the kitchen where she washed them and left them on the sink to drain. Then she drifted through the darkened house towards the room she'd prepared for the baby.

She was proud of the mural of brightly coloured sea creatures she'd created along one wall and she'd continued the theme with a sea horse and starfish mobile. The remaining walls were sand-coloured, the carpet a soft blue like the sea on a summer's day and the furnishings were the crisp white of foam-tipped waves.

Running her hand along the glossy white rail of the cot, she tried to picture her baby curled up asleep.

Thinking about her baby boy, rather than his father, Meg felt calmer again. Through the window, she could see the river, where the moonlight spread its luminescent glow across the silken black water. This was a nice little home for him to grow up in. They would be happy here.

She and her little boy would be close, just as she'd been with her father. She blocked out other memories of her childhood: when she'd longed to be part of a larger family—with two parents and some brothers or sisters.

Lifting her arms to her hair, she removed the elastic

band and pins and shook her curls free. She turned to walk down the passage to her bedroom. But she had only taken three steps, when she felt a cramp, low in her belly.

And the next minute her tights were all wet.

Sam pushed open the heavy glass doors of his hotel and made his way across the foyer. In the time he'd taken to drive from Meg's he hadn't cooled down any, so he could look forward to another sleepless night.

'Mr Kirby?' A woman at the reception desk beckoned to him. 'Someone's on the line asking for you. Been trying to call you for the past ten minutes.'

Sam nodded. 'I'll take the call in my room.'

Frowning, the woman raised a frayed fingernail to her lips and gave it a hurried chew. 'Actually, maybe you should take it here. She sounds kind of desperate.'

'She?' In two strides he was at the counter almost grabbing the receiver out of the woman's hand. 'Hello.'

'Sam?' Meg's voice sounded tiny.

'Meg, what is it?'

'You turned off your mobile.'

He grabbed the machine from his hip pocket. 'I turned it off at the class. But anyway, why have you rung?'

'My water's broken.'

A jolt of adrenaline rushed through him so fast he had to grab the desk for support. Slapping his hand over the mouthpiece, he whispered to the receptionist, 'Her waters have broken.'

The woman's eyes bulged. 'She's needs to get to a hospital straight away.'

'You need to get to a hospital straight away,' he told Meg.

'I know that, Sam.'

'Can you hold on till I get back to your place?'

'I—I guess so. Yes. I'm sure I can.'

'OK. I'm coming, sweetheart. Listen, the mobile's back on now. We can keep in contact while I'm on my way. Hang up and I'll ring you back.'

He almost threw the receiver at the receptionist and dashed back out through the hotel doors to the car park. Once he had his car heading back down the highway towards Meg's place, he phoned her. 'How you doing?'

'OK. I'm getting contractions.'

'Are they strong?'

'Fairly. About three minutes apart.'

'Three minutes!' Sweat broke out all over Sam. 'Maybe we should get an ambulance.'

'I'd rather wait for you.'

He accelerated. 'Are you remembering to relax?' he managed to ask. 'Are you doing your deep breathing?'

There was a silence at the other end.

'Meg?'

'No, I haven't been very relaxed,' she said and he thought she sounded weepy. 'I guess I panicked.'

'That's OK, honey,' he murmured, as he manoeuvred a sudden curve. 'You can do it, now. Do it just like you did at the class tonight. You're terrific at it.'

'Yes,' she whispered. 'Thanks. I forgot. Oh, there's another one coming.'

He heard a little gasp and then the sound of deep, slow breathing. 'That sounds real good, Nutmeg.' He pulled up at traffic lights, his stomach a bunch of knots. This baby was coming a few weeks early. He hoped like crazy everything was all right. Pounding his fist against the steering wheel, he cursed the red light. 'Change, damn you! I can't hang around all night.'

'Sam?' Meg's voice came through again.

'I'm right here. How are you?'

'A lot better. Thanks for reminding me to breathe. I forgot all about it, I was so scared.'

The lights changed and he took off once more, taking full advantage of his sports car's ability to duck and weave through the traffic, while cursing the fact that they drove on the wrong side of the road down under. 'That's what I'm here for,' he replied, trying to sound a whole heap calmer than he felt. 'Now, do you have your hospital bag packed and ready?'

'Yes.'

'Good girl.'

'Are you comfortable?'

'Hardly. I feel like I've got a coconut pressing down inside me.'

'That'll be the baby's head. That's good, Meg. It means everything is at it should be.' Where he'd got that information from, Sam wasn't sure, but it seemed to reassure Meg.

'Where are you, Sam? How long do you think you'll be?'

'I'm about ten minutes away.'

'OK. Oh—oh!'

The breathing started again and Sam took a deep breath in sympathy. He could feel his own gut squeezing tight. He hadn't prayed in a while, but he suddenly sent a silent plea for Meg and a quick request for strength for himself. No wonder Meg was frightened. He was absolutely terrified.

Again, he wondered if he should be dialing for an ambulance, but decided for the time being to take his cue from Meg. From what he'd read, first babies usually took their time coming. And besides, she wanted *him*! His heart swelled with an uplift of emotion.

Meg's voice came through again. 'Oh, boy, that was a stronger one.'

'You still OK?'

'Yes, but I can't wait to see you.'

Despite his anxiety, he smiled.

'Oh, no. There's another one already. Oh, Sa-a-am!'

The anguish in her cry sent panic surging like a tidal wave through Sam. He was hot and cold at once. 'Stay calm, darling. Just breathe. Come on, now—calming breaths. You can do it.'

Suddenly, he didn't care about safety. He slammed his foot down on the accelerator and charged towards Meg's place with his heart in his mouth. In the background, all he could hear were her desperate whimpers and sobs coming over the phone. She sounded so distressed, he wanted to kill someone.

It occurred to him in a blinding flash that, if anything happened to Meg now, he might do something really reckless. *He loved her!*

Tom had told Dolly she'd given his life shape and splendour. Now he understood what the old guy had meant. Without Meg, Sam knew his life would be empty and worthless.

After what seemed like an endless, frustrating maze of right and left turns, his tyres screeched as he roared to a halt outside her house. Luckily, she'd left the front door unlocked and Sam sprinted inside, shouting as he ran, 'Meg! Where are you?'

There was no answer.

CHAPTER TEN

'MEG!' Sam shouted, dashing and skidding through the house, checking rooms as he ran. Every nightmare, every fear he'd ever dealt with paled to nothing beside the overwhelming terror that seized him now.

Her bedroom was at the back of the house, but at last he found her. Curled on her side, she was in the middle of the bed, her golden hair in disarray and her face bleached white with fear. She was clutching at a bed sheet.

'Meg,' he whispered. 'What's happening?'

She couldn't answer. Suddenly her face screwed up in pain and her body stiffened.

'Hey, sweetheart,' he whispered. 'It's OK. I'll get you to the hospital. Try to relax. Breathe for me. You can do it.'

She shook her head and tears rolled down her cheeks. Sam felt a painful sob rising in his throat. Somehow he held it back.

On one reckless night last May, he'd made passionate love to this beautiful woman and now she was in agony. All because of him.

At last the contraction seemed to be over.

'I think I'm in transition,' Meg whispered. 'I feel awful. Oh, Sam. I'm so scared.'

Transition! From what he'd read, that meant the baby would be arriving soon.

'Let me carry you to the car.'

'No!' she wailed. 'Don't move me. *Please!* I can't move.'

'I'm going to call an ambulance,' he told her.

This time she didn't object.

Snatching the phone out of his pocket, he began to punch in numbers, but he was hit by sudden confusion. 'What's the number for emergencies in Australia?'

'Triple zero,' Meg whispered urgently through gritted teeth.

Once again he punched the numbers.

'Oh, no! Oh, no! Sam, I think the baby's com-i-i-ing!'

Coming? It couldn't be! His heart slammed against his ribs. Babies weren't supposed to come this fast! 'Hold on, Meg!' he cried, shocked to the core by the signs of strain in her face.

'I ca-a-n't,' she cried back. 'I've got to push!'

'Hello,' said a voice in Sam's ear. 'Which department did you want, ambulance, fire or police?'

'Ambulance!' he shouted.

'Sa-a-am! Help me-e!'

Meg looked terrified.

'Ambulance service. How can I help you?'

Panic stricken, Sam yelled, 'We're at thirty-seven Casurina Drive. There's a baby coming! Get here fast!'

He threw down the phone and crouched close to Meg. She had rolled onto her back and her eyes were dilated with fear. He was frightened too. He had no idea how long it would take for the ambulance to arrive.

'It's coming, Sam.' She sobbed. 'We don't have time to go anywhere. I think I'm going to have it any minute now. I'm so scared! Don't leave me.'

'I'm not going anywhere, Nutmeg. I'm staying right here to help you. Are you comfortable like that?'

'I guess I need to—o-oh!'

Once more her face crumpled. He could see the strain in her neck as she began to bear down again.

'Don't fight it,' Sam murmured, hoping his advice was correct. 'Go with the pain. I guess you may as well push. You can do it.'

In a little while, she relaxed back against the pillows, looking flushed, but calmer.

'Let me get you more comfortable.' There was a glass of water on her night table. 'Would you like a sip of water?'

She nodded and he lifted her head to take a little drink.

When she began to grunt with another contraction, he sat beside her, supporting her back, helping her to lean into the urge to push, just as they'd practised a few hours before.

'You're fantastic, Meg!'

'How am I doing down the business end?' She nodded to her lower regions.

He moved down the bed, more than a little scared about what he would find. 'It's just great! It looks just like in the movie at the class.' He managed a crooked grin. 'Only better.'

Her mouth quirked into the tiniest of smiles and Sam stepped forward and kissed her cheek. Somewhere, amid the panic that rioted inside him, he managed to think that she'd never looked more beautiful.

'I didn't mean to have the baby at home,' she said with another sob. 'Oh!' She let forth a swear word Sam hadn't realised she used and, once again, she began to bear down. A loud, grunting groan burst from her lips.

'I can see the baby's head, Meg!' Sam called suddenly and he felt tears of panic, excitement and joy clogging his throat and welling in his eyes. 'He's got black hair.'

Meg smiled through her pain. After a moment's respite, she panted. 'Black—that's good!'

Sam shot a frantic glance through the bedroom window to the street outside. His heart raced as if he'd swum clear across the Pacific.

Slow down, baby!

Where's that ambulance? he wanted to scream but, for Meg's sake, he kept quiet, hiding his fright. What on earth would he do if the baby kept coming and he was here on his own? Facing a tiger shark on the bottom of the ocean would be a piece of cake compared to this.

But he didn't have any choice. The contractions were forcing Meg to push again and the baby's head was moving slowly forward. Sam gulped. 'You go, girl!' he whispered. 'He's looking great.'

'Oh—oh!' Meg cried. She dragged in another deep breath and began to push once more.

'His head is on the way out!' Sam told her. 'I can see his forehead. Here come his eyes…his nose!' His heart clattered in his chest as he stared at the tiny head. It was wrinkled and wet and dark. 'I'd say he's kinda cute-looking.'

Red-faced, Meg managed another quick smile before she began another push. She was looking tired and he raced to prop her back with more pillows. Then he darted to check on the baby's progress. The shoulders were emerging. The baby seemed to be turning slightly. He rubbed his hands nervously together, took a deep breath and grasped his son's tiny shoulders.

To his amazement, the little guy continued to progress forward without any assistance. Smart kid! All Sam needed to do was be there. Soon the rest of the shiny body was slipping away from Meg and into his hands.

Awestruck, he held his son, as his little arms and legs

flung wide. Through a throat choked with emotion, Sam managed to cry, 'He's here, Meg! You have your little boy.'

At the sound of her cry of triumph, a new fear clutched at Sam. What in heaven's name was he supposed to do now? The tiny body in his hands was slippery and wet. The kid looked incredibly like a startled frog. Meg had done her part. Was this where he was supposed to spank the poor little guy? In the movie, they did medical-type things like suctioning out the baby's nose and throat.

Sam felt a primal male urge to get the hell out of there.

Suddenly, the little arms flew wide open again and a lusty, 'Waa' erupted from the baby's mouth. His tiny face grew red as his cries gained volume. 'Thank God!' Sam breathed.

A relief such as he'd never known before, flooded through him. Relief! Elation! Overwhelming love. An urge to shout from rooftops! A dozen emotions shook him.

'My baby!' cried Meg. 'Let me see him.'

With intense concentration, he gently lifted the little fellow onto her stomach. 'Here you are, you clever girl.'

'Oh, Sam, he's beautiful.'

'He's perfect,' Sam agreed, blinking his eyes, but not really caring about tears any more. This little creature with a scrunched-up face was the most perfect kid in the whole world.

He sat beside Meg and helped to support her so she could see the little miracle she'd produced.

'He's a funny colour,' she whispered. 'But I think brand new babies look like that.'

'He's fine, honey. He's getting pinker by the minute.'

'Look at his little hands. His tiny fingers. Oh, his eyes are open.' Little black eyes blinked at them. 'Sam.' She sobbed. 'He's gorgeous.' Through her tears, Meg looked up at him. 'Thank you,' she whispered.

Now it was over, he was shaking. 'Hey, you did it all by yourself. You were fantastic.' He kissed her forehead and tenderly brushed damp curls from her face. 'You were so brave.' Clearing his throat, he added, 'Am I— are we supposed to do anything about the cord?'

'The ambulance should be here soon. They'll look after it,' Meg responded. Now that she had her baby, she didn't seem to be worried about anything else.

Their son began to cry again and Meg stroked his back gently. 'He feels so soft,' she whispered.

'Maybe we should keep him warm.'

'There's a baby blanket in my bag.' She pointed to a suitcase standing near the doorway.

'I'll get it and then I'll check again where the ambulance has got to.' Sam flipped open the locks on the case and sorted through the neatly folded items. He found a soft white blanket dotted with tiny blue sea horses. Smiling, he covered the baby and Meg.

There was a knock at the door.

'That'll be the ambulance.' He dropped another kiss on her warm cheek and stood up, calling loudly, 'We're in here!'

Meg smiled at him and she looked as if she would be smiling from now until Christmas.

Meg lay in her hospital bed and stared at the tiny form in the crib beside her. A tiny pink and perfect face topped by thick black hair peeped out of a neatly bundled bunny rug.

It's all over! her mind kept repeating. *I have a baby and he's fine! He's beautiful!* She had never known such exhilaration. Such a sense of achievement.

She had never known such love. She was bursting with goodwill towards the entire universe. Love for the baby. Love for Sam. Especially for Sam.

Where was he?

Once the ambulance had arrived, there had been so much action. And when they'd got to the hospital, people had kept buzzing continuously around her, doing things to her and the baby. There had been a constant flow of people checking one medical detail or another and Sam had disappeared into the background. Even when she'd been settled into this private room, which he'd insisted she must have, the nurses had sent him away so she could rest.

But she'd rested all night and now she wanted him. She needed him.

Sam had delivered her baby! The very thought filled her with awe. He'd been magnificent. Without him, she would have been a screaming, sobbing mess!

And afterwards! The three of them—Sam, herself and their little boy—it had been a moment of such closeness. An experience of bonding beyond her wildest dreams.

There was a telephone on her bedside table and, impulsively, she decided to dial his mobile.

'Sam Kirby.'

'Hi there, Daddy.'

'Meg! Are you OK?'

'Wonderful,' she whispered back. 'Where are you?'

'In the hospital foyer, wondering whether I should visit you so early.'

Meg found she was grinning. 'Get right up here at once,' she ordered.

'I'm on my way.'

She slipped the telephone receiver gently into its cradle and sank back onto the pillows, satisfied.

Within minutes, Sam's tall dark frame appeared in the doorway. He carried a huge bunch of roses.

'How did you know I love pink roses?' Meg asked, delighted. Everything seemed delightful on this wonderful day.

'Oh, I can be quite intuitive at times.' He smiled down at her. 'You look really well, Meg.' He reached down to lightly brush her cheek. 'I guess radiant would be the right word.'

'I'm on top of the world.' She sighed happily.

He settled on the side of the bed nearest the baby and peered into the crib. 'Doesn't he look different now he's all scrubbed up and wearing clothes?'

'I have to keep telling myself he's real. Isn't he the best looking baby you've ever seen?'

'My experience doesn't count for much. The only brand-new creatures I've met at close quarters have been puppies and guppies.' Sam studied his son and then grinned at Meg. 'But, yeah, he's a great looking guy.'

'He looks just like you.'

Sam shook his head and laughed.

After a moment of silence, while they both gazed at the sleeping baby, Meg reached out with one finger and touched the back of Sam's hand where it rested on the counterpane. 'I'm so grateful for the way you helped me.'

Rolling his hand over, he captured hers and squeezed. 'All part of the service, ma'am.'

His eyes held a soft glow that snaffled Meg's breath. She dropped her gaze and gently removed her hand from his grasp.

'What are you planning to call him?' Sam asked.

Meg took a deep breath. 'Tom.'

'Tom?' he repeated, sounding shaken. 'After my grandfather?'

'He would never have been born if it wasn't for your grandfather's letter in the bottle,' she said softly. 'I was thinking I'd like to call him Thomas Samuel.'

An emotion Meg couldn't identify tightened Sam's face. He got to his feet quickly and, staring down, shoved his hands in his pockets.

'You have any objection?' she asked cautiously.

'No.' He shook his head. 'No, they're fine names. They go well with—with your name—Bennet. Thomas Samuel Bennet. It sounds—solid.'

Meg's eyes misted. She didn't know where her ridiculous brain had been trailing but, somewhere in the past hours, between the baby's birth and this moment, she'd stopped thinking about a future without Sam.

She pressed four fingers to her lips. Soon, he would be heading back to Seattle.

'Can I hold him for a moment?' Sam asked.

'Sure,' she said and bit her lip as he bent over the cot and gently picked up his sleeping son. Tom looked so tiny in his father's big strong arms. You mustn't get weepy, she lectured herself. But the tears came anyway. She couldn't help it.

And Sam looked so cute standing there, holding the tiny bundle in his big hands and looking down into the baby's sleeping face. He stared intently, as if he were imprinting every detail to store up memories.

'Well, Tom,' he said softly, 'I dare say you won't always be as angelic as you look right at this moment, but I want you to be a good kid for your mom. Do you hear me, bud?' His glance stole swiftly in Meg's direction and, when he saw her tears, he frowned. 'Are you OK?'

Snatching up a tissue, she blotted her face and blew her nose. 'Just feeling a bit emotional.'

'You must still be tired. I should head off soon.'

'Will you come and visit us later?'

Sam's face darkened and, bending over the crib, he placed the baby down once more. 'I don't think so.'

'Oh?' Meg tried not to sound disappointed, but failed miserably.

He straightened and folding his arms over his chest, eyed her steadily. 'We have a deal, remember. You made me promise not to hang around once the little guy arrived safely.'

'But I—I didn't think you'd want to get away this quickly.'

His jaw jutted forward as he stood considering her words. He spoke to the opposite wall. 'Hanging around now isn't going to help anybody.' Slowly he swung his gaze to look her in the eye.

Meg's mind twisted and turned, trying to make sense of her sudden misery. Sam was right. She'd made him promise not to make a nuisance of himself once the baby was born. Yesterday, this arrangement had seemed the perfect solution. A wonderful idea. Of course, she hadn't expected Tom to arrive so soon.

What a difference a day could make.

She was tempted to blurt out that she'd changed her mind—that she wanted him to stay. Surely everything was different now? They'd been through so much together. But somewhere in the back of her head a little niggle of common sense warned against making a rash decision.

He sighed. 'If I'm going to head off, I'd prefer to do it sooner rather than later.'

It was hard to sort out her feelings right at this moment, but she knew she might regret saying or doing anything on an impulsive whim. Over the past eight months she'd planned exactly how she wanted her life to be. She'd be foolish to change her mind in just eight hours.

Her lips trembled as she whispered, 'Are you going straight back to Seattle?'

He didn't answer at first. He stood looking at her, his eyes searching her face as if trying to read the turmoil of thoughts she kept hidden. Finally, he said, 'I thought I'd like to spend some more time up north. Probably on Magnetic Island. I want to take a really good look at the reef.'

Somehow, Meg felt better knowing that Sam would still be in Australia. But not much better.

'Meg, you made me promise I would go after the birth. You still want me to go, don't you?'

No! No she didn't want him to go anywhere. She wanted Sam right here, looking at Tom with her, agreeing with her that he was the most wonderful baby in the universe.

He thrust his hands deep in his pockets and let out a ragged sigh. 'Don't make this hard for me.'

She suspected she was being selfish again. Feeling vulnerable and emotional wasn't a good reason to cling to Sam. In a few days she'd feel stronger.

'You should go, Sam,' she said softly.

He quickly looked away. 'OK,' he said, sounding efficient.

'I'll keep in touch.'

'Good. That'll be—great.'

'I'll write and tell you what Tommy's doing.'

'Thanks. Yeah, I'd like to keep track of him.' He was looking at the highly waxed hospital floor as if something down there was fascinating him.

'I can send you photos.'

His head jerked up. 'Photos? Yeah. Good idea. I forgot

to bring a camera.' And then, without another word, he held his hand up in a funny little saluting sort of gesture and headed for the door.

Not even a kiss goodbye!

'Sam!' she called.

In the doorway, he swung back.

She knew he would stay if she asked him to. Just lately, he'd given the impression that he would do anything she asked…

Right this minute she didn't know what she wanted. Perhaps it would help if she asked him what *he* really wanted?

She sat up straighter, the question poised on her lips. But he looked so ready for flight, her courage faded. 'Take care,' she called.

He gave a curt nod and, the next minute, he was gone.

CHAPTER ELEVEN

SAM swam to the far end of Florence Bay to where the jumble of smooth basalt boulders met the sand. The afternoon sun was already slipping towards the western hills, taking the heat out of the day as it went. In a lazy overarm crawl, he turned, planning to head back for one more lap across the bay, when a seagull took off from a nearby rock with a sudden noisy shriek.

Sensing that something or someone must have startled the bird, he blinked salt water from his eyes as he looked towards the shore. But the beach was empty.

It was a weird thought, but he could have sworn that someone had been there. Shrugging, he set off again, churning across the bay once more, just as he had every afternoon for the past six weeks.

These days, he was free to do exactly what he wanted whenever he wanted. It was the kind of freedom he'd craved when he'd been chained to a desk at Kirby & Son, but now he found his freedom had a bitter edge. It wasn't quite the blissful life he'd imagined. Of course, in time, he'd feel better.

When he'd stopped thinking about Meg and Tom.

After another lap, he could feel the familiar ache in his muscles that told him he'd pushed himself far enough for this session. He liked to stretch his body to the point of exhaustion. It made sleep come more easily. Turning for the shore, he let a small wave carry him into the shallows and then he stood and walked towards his towel.

A strand of seaweed clung to his chest and he flicked it off.

Out of the corner of his eye, he saw it land on a bottle sticking half in, half out of the sand.

The humid March air closed in and dark clouds along the horizon hinted at a hovering storm. Peeling his stinger suit down, Sam towelled himself dry then hauled on an old pair of track-suit bottoms.

The bottle, draped in seaweed, caught his eye once more as he bent over to recover his towel. For a ridiculous moment, he had a fanciful notion that there was something inside the bottle.

Like a piece of paper.

But that kind of coincidence didn't happen in real life. Without giving it another thought, he snatched up the towel and began to jog along the beach towards the car park.

One more time he looked back at the bottle, but the shadows were lengthening across the sand and all he could see now was a dark blob. With a shrug, he headed for his car.

Meg felt so much better now she'd finally come back and had booked into a holiday cottage at Magnetic Rendezvous. Her little house on the Sunshine Coast had been fine but, ever since Sam had decided to stay on in Australia, she'd felt a force drawing her inevitably to the north.

She tucked little Tom into his basket and covered him with a light cotton blanket. Considering the state of her nerves, she was amazed he'd fallen asleep so quickly and easily this evening.

Leaving a night light burning, she tiptoed out of the room and headed for the mirror in the bathroom to check her hair and make-up. She was pleased with what she saw. Apart from the fact that her breasts were fuller, there weren't any obvious signs that she'd recently had a baby. The white trousers and silky knit top she wore tonight were ones she'd been able to wear in pre-pregnancy days.

Leaning closer to her reflection, she touched up her lipstick and dabbed a little extra scent to her wrists.

In the tiny kitchen, a chicken casserole was simmering in the oven. A chilled bottle of white wine, a bowl of green salad and a cheese platter waited in the fridge. Everything was ready. She looked at her watch. If her plan had worked, she calculated that Sam should be knocking on her door any minute now.

Once again, she checked the table setting. The little bowl of brown and yellow bush orchids looked just right as a centre-piece. The lamps in the lounge were casting a welcoming glow across the small room.

Perhaps she should turn the oven down just a fraction, to prevent the chicken from getting too brown on top? Again she checked her watch.

She decided to turn the television on and to try to act as if she wasn't desperately waiting for him. She flipped through the channels. News...more news...sport...a games show. She couldn't pay attention to any of them this evening. All she could think about was Sam...and what she would say to him when he came...

Fifteen minutes later, she began to wonder if he had seen the bottle! She had placed it close to his towel and she was sure that he would find it there but, perhaps, by some quirk of fate, he'd walked straight past.

Now, she wished she'd stayed on the beach, but it had been threatening to rain and she'd been worried that Tom would get caught in a storm, or that Sam might have seen her. That would have spoiled the surprise and ruined her plan.

Another possibility seized her. Sam could have seen the bottle, read her message and disregarded it. That thought was unbearable.

Surely her beautiful plan wasn't about to fall flat on its face?

Meg's optimism faltered. If he still hadn't come after another five minutes, she would ring through to the helpful woman in reception—the new woman called Ellen, with the American accent.

In the shower, Sam flexed his shoulders and let the hot water stream over his back, releasing the tension in his muscles. It felt good.

Idly, he picked up the soap and began to lather his chest. He let his mind drift as he relaxed some more and, unexpectedly, the weirdest thought struck him. It came so suddenly that the soap slipped from his hand and slithered to the floor. His head shot up and he stared at the water pinging off the tiles.

He'd seen an image of that bottle in the sand again.

And it hit him, out of the blue, that the bottle hadn't been there when he'd first arrived at the beach. He had a perfectly clear picture of walking onto the beach and tossing his towel down on the sand. It had been a bare stretch of sand. A perfectly bare patch.

And yet when he'd come out of the water, there had been a bottle right next to his towel.

He tried for calm as he turned off the taps, but wild thoughts persisted.

When he'd been swimming, he'd sensed someone was there on the beach. He remembered the seagull's startled reaction. Now, he was sure someone *had* been there.

And that someone had left a bottle near his towel.

Trying to tone down his sense of agitation, he quickly dried himself and hauled on a T-shirt, jeans and trainers. In the kitchen drawer, he found a torch. Maybe he was going crazy, but it was suddenly incredibly important to get back to the bay straight away and find that bottle.

'I'm sorry,' the woman from reception told Meg. 'Mr. Kirby doesn't seem to be in. I've rung his unit several times, but there's no answer.'

'Thank you. Maybe I'll try again later.' Meg let the receiver drop.

What a prime idiot she was.

She'd been totally carried away by a romantic fantasy! Over the past six weeks, her feelings for Sam had become so powerful, so overflowing, that she hadn't been able to hold back any longer. She'd reached the point where she had to find a way to win him back.

When she came up with the wonderful, superbly romantic idea of sending Sam a message in a bottle, she'd been so pleased with herself.

Now, as she wandered listlessly into the kitchen and turned off the oven, she realised it was an impractical, pathetic idea. *A drippy, desperate, downright dumb idea.* Maternal hormones must have withered her brain.

Snatching up oven gloves, she lifted the casserole dish out of the oven and set it on a tiled mat to cool. Two huge, fat tears plopped onto its lid and sizzled.

She'd been so foolish. Like a dizzy balloon that had lost its air, she felt totally deflated and empty. All day she'd floated on excitement. Her energy had been fuelled by such high hopes. She'd flown up from Brisbane, had travelled across to the island on the ferry, had dashed around frantically preparing dinner, had raced down to the beach with the stupid bottle...

And now...

Disappointment was such an exhausting emotion!

She didn't feel like eating, or removing her make-up. Suddenly, all she wanted was to curl up in bed and howl herself to sleep.

'Ellen, has anyone been trying to contact me?' Sam panted as he dashed into reception, frantic with frustration. By the time he'd reached the bay, the tide had come in and had completely covered the sand. He hadn't been able to find the bottle anywhere.

And now he was desperate.

His receptionist looked up, surprised. 'There you are, Sam. Yes, a young woman has been very anxious about your whereabouts.'

'Young woman?' he repeated, seriously short of breath and not because he'd been running.

'Meg Bennet,' Ellen elaborated, her wide eyes speaking volumes. 'Didn't you know she's booked into unit sixteen?'

'Oh?' Sam responded, suddenly trying to sound casual, while shock waves jolted and ricocheted through him. *Meg was here on the island?* His heart pounded as he glanced at his watch and lifted one shoulder in an attempt at a careless shrug. 'I guess she'd be asleep by now. No doubt she'll contact me in the morning if she really wants me.'

He managed to make his way back out of reception at a normal walking pace, but once he hit the pathway leading to the bungalows, Sam sprinted.

Unit sixteen was in total darkness.

He stared at the black cabin and the curtained windows

and groaned. Meg was inside! She'd been trying to reach him. Knowing that, how could he wait all night? He walked up to the door and thought about knocking. She wouldn't appreciate it if he woke the baby. Heaving a heavy sigh, he turned away again.

But damn it. How could he give up? It was *Meg* inside. Seconds later, he knocked on the door, not worried if he woke the entire resort. 'Meg,' he called, 'are you there?'

From inside the cottage, he could hear little bumps and thuds as if someone was stumbling in the dark. Then footsteps. A light came on. He tried to calm his breathing as the door opened.

Dressed in an oversized button-through T-shirt, Meg peered out at him through red and swollen eyes, ringed with smudged make-up.

'Sam?' she whispered. 'Is it you?'

'Yes. I—er—believe you've been trying to contact me.'

'I have.' Her voice sounded squeaky with surprise.

'I thought maybe there was something wrong with the baby. Is he OK?'

'Yes, yes, he's fine. I—I wasn't expecting you to come now. It's late.' One hand darted to her dishevelled curls while the other clutched at her nightdress.

It occurred to Sam that any other girl would look terrible, but Meg still managed to look graceful and sexy.

'I'm sorry if I've woken you up.'

'No, you didn't.' She hesitated. 'Do you want to come in?'

'Sure.'

Meg looked a little confused but, after another slight hesitation, stepped back to allow him through the door.

'Crumbs,' she muttered half to herself, 'I must look a fright.' She turned and cast him an embarrassed smile over her shoulder. 'Can you give me a minute to wash my face?'

'Of course,' Sam agreed.

She disappeared and he was left to pace the room, feeling jittery and nervous, as if he was about to sit for an important test without any preparation. He didn't have a clue why Meg was here on the island. It was obvious she'd been crying but, if he let his brain try to come up with reasons, he feared he would go crazy.

She looked like a racoon with hay fever! Meg scrubbed furiously at her face. What a disaster! She'd so wanted to look nice for Sam. Everything was supposed to be perfect—the meal, the flowers, the clothes. She patted her skin dry and brushed her hair quickly. The black rings were gone from around her eyes, but she still looked pale and strained.

She sent her reflection a hopeful smile. It would have to do. Sam wouldn't appreciate being kept waiting.

In the lounge, he was looking grim and frowning. She'd been hoping for a relaxed and pleasant evening, not more worry and tension! Taking a seat, she gestured for him to sit down, too.

As he did so, her eyes honed in hungrily on all the things she loved about Sam—his dreamy blue eyes, the sheen of his hair in the lamp light, the shape of his hands—well, all of him really. He was looking tanned and very fit and his hair had grown longer. Living on the island suited him.

'I guess you're surprised to see me here,' she said shyly.

He nodded.

She felt awkward, not sure where to begin her explanation.

'How's Tom?' he asked.

'He's fine.'

'Has he grown much?'

'Heaps. Would you like to see him?'

'Ah—yeah. That'd be great.'

Jumping back out of her chair, she led him down the short passage to the bedroom. In the glow of the night light, little Tom lay snuggled on his side with a chubby pink hand curled close to his mouth. His head was covered by a downy cap of dark hair. A little bubble of milk rested on his lower lip and he pouted gently in his sleep. Meg smiled, enjoying the warm glow of motherly love that was so much a part of her life these days.

She looked up at Sam.

'He's so much fatter,' he murmured.

'He certainly has his priorities figured out,' Meg agreed. 'Food's the most important thing in his life at the moment.'

'That's the trick, bud,' he murmured. 'Don't let your life get too complicated.'

They exchanged self-conscious smiles and tiptoed back outside.

Once more they sat in separate chairs, facing each other a little awkwardly.

Glancing to the darkened kitchen, Meg said quickly, 'I cooked dinner, but it'll probably be cold now.'

'You cooked dinner? You were expecting me for dinner?'

She sighed. 'It was a really silly idea. I put a message in a bottle and left it on the beach near your towel. I guess you didn't notice it.'

'So there *was* a message in that bottle,' he said softly, almost to himself.

'As I said, it was a stupid idea. One of those things that seem brilliant when you first think of them...'

'By the time it occurred to me that there might be a message, I'm afraid the tide was in. I couldn't find the bottle.'

Meg rubbed one bare foot against the other. 'You went back tonight looking for it? Oh, boy! I've really botched things up.'

He leaned forward in his chair, linking his hands loosely between his knees and her heart turned over when he sent her one of his slow, lazy smiles. 'Maybe things aren't all that botched. I'm here now. Tell me now whatever you wanted to say.'

She gulped. 'I spent ages trying to write that note—getting the wording right. There are so many things I wanted to explain.'

Sam cocked his head to one side. 'I'm a good listener.'

It was probably now or never, but Meg wished her stomach wasn't jumping around like a grasshopper trapped in a jar. 'Well, I wanted to explain that maybe I was sorry I sent you away so quickly.'

He didn't say anything, just sat there watching her, waiting for her to finish her explanation.

Anxiously, Meg wetted her lips with her tongue. She felt sick with nerves and her hands clenched into tight fists. She wanted so badly for Sam to hold her. 'I should have given you a chance to tell me how *you* felt—about—everything,' she cried. 'I was so busy worrying about myself. But, Sam, what you did for Tommy and me—the night he was born. It—it was just so special.'

She was grateful that she managed to keep tears out of her voice, but he was staring at her with such fierce concentration Meg's courage almost faltered. Feeling flustered, she pushed herself out of her chair and began to pace the room. 'I've been thinking over what you said—about how we didn't get to know each other by the usual route. Everything happened so quickly and we didn't give ourselves the chance to understand each other. We need to fill in the gaps in our relationship.'

His eyebrows rose.

'And so I thought that while you're still hanging around on the island—' She paused for a minute and frowned at him. 'Why *are* you still here, Sam? Aren't you'd supposed to be back in Seattle by now?'

'We'll get to that later. Tell me more about your plans for our relationship.'

'So you're interested?'

'Mildly.'

'I see.' Meg's cheeks flamed and her throat felt very parched.

Sam rose too and stood looking at her with a disturbing glimmer in his eyes. 'Meg, I was teasing. I'm sorry. The truth is I'm exceedingly interested in anything you have to say about us.'

She swallowed.

'What did you have in mind?' he asked in a husky voice.

'I think it really would be an excellent idea if I tried to get to know my baby's father better.'

A smile spread slowly to reach his eyes. Meg's stomach grew even more jittery as he began to walk towards her. Just out of reach, he stopped and their eyes locked.

Her voice was a breathy whisper. 'You told me you do getting-to-know-you best face to face. That's why I came.'

Reaching out, he took her hand. 'And you told me I was even better at mouth-to-mouth.'

He drew her closer and, with one hand lifting her chin,

his face lowered towards hers. 'Just a taste test,' he whispered, as he lightly nibbled her lower lip.

'Taste as much as you like,' she whispered back.

'Don't worry, I plan to.' He took her hand in his and he rubbed his thumb slowly back and forth over her knuckles. 'But tell me a little more about why you're here.'

Meg swallowed again. 'This is how it's been with us, isn't it? We've been through some amazing times together.' She felt her cheeks warm. 'Making babies—delivering babies. We seem to be quite good at the big moments.'

'We're *great* at the big moments, Meg.'

'I got around to thinking maybe we could be good at the little things, too.'

'Like becoming friends?'

'Yes. We could keep it low-key if you like—just one step at a time.'

'Low-key,' he repeated, his voice rumbling with an unreadable emotion. His thumb stopped moving. He frowned as he looked down at her. 'Please don't tell me you want to go through all those rules again?'

'Rules?'

'You can't have forgotten. If we kiss the lips have to stay tight shut. No touching certain...'

'Actually, no.' Meg felt frumpy talking about such details in her old nightdress, but it couldn't be helped. Sam had seen her looking worse. 'If I'm honest, I don't want that kind of low-key at all.'

'That's a relief.'

She drew in a deep breath. 'The absolute truth is, I—' she took another breath '—I've had all these arguments going on in my head about why I should stay away from you. But they're losing out. My heart's winning hands down. I love you, Sam.'

'You're sure about that?' he whispered.

'I thought I was sure about it last year, but I *know* I've been sure about it for the past six weeks.' Her throat was so choked with tears she could hardly get the words out. An embarrassing sob broke through and, when she spoke again, the tears flowed. 'I've reached the point where I want you so badly I can't think about anything else.'

'Oh, sweetheart.'

His arms closed tightly around her and she sobbed against the soft ribbed cotton of his T-shirt. Beneath it she could feel the rock-hard strength of his shoulders and chest.

'So, now you know.' She squeaked the words out. 'I expressed it a lot better in the letter.'

'Nutmeg, you couldn't have said it any better,' he murmured against her cheek. 'There are no better words the world over.' His warm lips kissed her forehead, her tear-stained cheek and her damp eyelids.

With an embarrassed little smile, Meg raised her eyes to meet his. 'I sent you away, and now here I am throwing myself at you.'

'Keep at it,' Sam murmured. 'You're doing a great job.'

Feeling braver, she scattered greedy kisses over his stubble-roughened jaw. 'Before I throw myself too far, perhaps I should do a bit more about getting to know you.'

'What would you like to know?'

'How long do you plan to stay here on the island?'

'I'm going to be here for ages. You see—' he smiled down at her and with one finger brushed a wisp of hair from her cheek '—I've bought the place.'

'You've bought Magnetic Rendezvous?'

'Yeah.'

'You've got to be joking.' She shook her head in bewilderment. 'Why?'

'Two reasons.' He kissed the tip of her nose. 'You're one.' He kissed her chin. 'And Tom's the other.'

Meg's heart fluttered wildly in her chest. 'But, Sam, I thought you were a hotshot businessman. I don't know if this place is a viable proposition. Fred never seemed to make much money. Did you check it out properly?'

'I've run a complete survey. It will be a runaway success by the time I've finished with it. I've big plans for an eco-friendly resort—a marine studies centre. It's the kind of challenge I've always dreamed of taking on.'

'Wow! That sounds brilliant. But what about Kirby & Son?'

'We've sold it.'

'My goodness.' Meg was flabbergasted.

'I'll explain more later,' he murmured, gathering her close again. 'Right now, there are more important things to consider.'

'Did you want—?'

He spoke into her hair. 'I only want to think about us. You and me and Tom. Look at me, Meg.'

When she looked into his sexy blue gaze, his eyes were so filled with emotion, her legs threatened to give way.

'Right now, I want to concentrate on you.' With parted lips, he drew a sweet, slow caress over her mouth. 'I want to tell you over and over how much I love you.'

'Oh, Sam,' Meg whispered.

'It hit me the night Tom came along, that I've been in love with you for months and months. I think it probably happened when I first met you, but I was slow to catch on. It nearly killed me to drag myself away from you when you were in hospital.'

She frowned. 'But you did it—'

'I did it because I loved you and it was what *you* wanted. When I realised I could put your needs before mine, that's when I knew for sure I was a goner.' He rubbed his chin in her hair as he held her closer. 'But I mustn't lose you again. I need you in my life, Meg.' His eyes smiled into hers. 'Every day.'

Meg's heart swelled. She couldn't speak.

But it didn't matter. Sam's strong arms were lifting her, carrying her across the room and then settling her onto his lap as he lowered himself onto the sofa.

Unable to restrain herself any longer, her hands began to explore the beautiful strength of his shoulders as her body arched against him. She buried her lips against the dark warmth of his neck, relishing the familiar smell and taste of his skin.

'Will you marry me, Nutmeg?' Sam's words feathered her cheek.

Yes! she wanted to cry, but her throat was so filled with happiness, her voice made no sound. But it didn't matter. She nodded and lifted her face so Sam could read her answer in her shining eyes.

And everything else that needed to be said was accomplished mouth to mouth.

EPILOGUE

EVERYTHING was so quiet as Sam Kirby walked through the open-plan living area of his home, that he wondered where his family was. Then he smiled when he saw Meg sitting with Dolly, out on the deck. They were enjoying the late afternoon breeze as it drifted up to them from the bay below.

When he pushed aside the sliding glass doors and stepped outside to join them, he realised the breeze wasn't the only thing drifting from below. The sounds of excited, girlish voices reached him.

'Our shell seekers are returning,' Dolly commented as he stooped to kiss her papery cheek.

'Hi there.' Meg reached up and squeezed his hand and she sent him a happy, welcoming smile. As always, when he kissed her, his heart responded with a little leap of joy.

The girls' cries became clearer. 'Granny Dolly, look at the pretty shell I found!'

'I got one, too!'

Sam looked in the direction of the voices. All that could be seen at this stage were two straw sun hats atop the two little girls, as they clambered up the cliff path towards the house. He chuckled. Beneath those look-alike shady hats, were his six-year-old twin daughters, Bella and Claire—as different as chalk and cheese.

Bella would be the one in front, bursting with impatience to show off her find, her round face flushed beneath a tumble of glossy, dark curls. Claire would be

182

following at a calmer pace, clutching her prize carefully, her thoughtful grey eyes peering from beneath a straight blonde fringe.

Taking a seat beside Meg, he draped an arm around her shoulders as they watched the girls reach the top of the cliff path and bound eagerly up the steps and onto the deck.

'Mine's a spotty shell.' Bella puffed, dropping a speck-led cowrie into Dolly's lap.

'It's beautiful, darling.' Dolly beamed.

Dolly's sprightliness continued to amaze Sam. Although she was ninety now, she didn't seem any older than when he'd first met her ten years ago.

'And what have you found, Claire?' the old lady was asking.

The other little girl placed a perfect, pink and white volute into Dolly's outstretched hand. He might have pre-dicted that Claire's shell would be less showy but just as beautiful as her sister's.

'This is lovely, too. It's so delicate. Aren't you both clever shell collectors?'

'They're for you,' Bella explained.

'Why, thank you so much. I'll find somewhere very special for them when I go home.' Dolly smiled at them both. 'I thought you might want to give these to Tom for his birthday.'

'He says shells are for girls,' Claire explained. 'He only collects sea-urchin skeletons.'

'Oh, I see.' Dolly sent Meg and Sam a knowing wink.

'He got a proper full wetsuit for his birthday, a weight belt and an underwater torch,' Bella elaborated. 'So he can go skin diving with Daddy.'

'Ten years' old! Tom really is growing up, isn't he?' Dolly sighed.

'That's what Mummy was saying this morning. She and Daddy were talking about when Tom was born,' Claire announced, and Meg and Sam exchanged smiles.

Bella, not to be beaten, added, 'But then Daddy started kissing Mummy—right in the middle of breakfast. Not just an ordinary kiss. A real long one.'

'Hey! Who's telling tales?' Sam laughed. He threaded his little finger into one of the wheat-coloured curls lying loose against Meg's neck. She turned and shot him a secret, sizzling smile. Luckily, his daughters didn't know the half of what he and their mother had been up to earlier this morning.

'They're not telling me anything I didn't already know,' remarked Dolly and her eyes misted.

Meg jumped to her feet. 'How about you girls go and look for your brother? It'll be time for his birthday tea soon. Just remind him we're having his favourites—lasagne and chocolate-layer cake.'

'I saw him down at the sea-horse tank,' Sam called after the girls as they eagerly headed off once more. To Meg, he commented, 'The staff have started calling Tom the apprentice, he spends so much time after school each day hanging about the research area.'

'He certainly loves the sea horses and he was so excited when they started breeding,' Meg agreed.

Dolly turned to them both. 'I meant what I said before. I'm so happy that you two have a very special marriage.' She smiled and her eyes glistened a little tearily. 'I know it might sound silly, but I've told my Tom about it and I know he's happy, too.'

'Oh, Dolly.' Meg stepped closer and took Dolly's hand in hers. 'We are just so grateful to your Tom. Sam and I would never have found each other without him. I'm sure he knew when he threw that bottle overboard that,

whatever happened, it would bring happiness, somewhere, some time.'

'Yes, I think that, too, dear.'

Sam switched his gaze to the horizon—to the Coral
Sea—where Tom had sailed and had not come back. It
always choked him up to think that his grandfather had
missed out on a happily married life, when his own was
so full and satisfactory in every way. Even his job was
fulfilling. Now he had the fun of making good money
while doing something he really loved.

Dolly's voice broke into his thoughts. 'I just feel so
blessed that I've been able to enjoy your little ones.'

'And you'll be able to enjoy them for another ten
years. You'll be here for your hundredth birthday, Dolly,'
Sam assured her. He jumped to his feet. 'Now, I'm going
to break open a bottle of champagne. You ladies will join
me in a celebration, won't you?'

'Of course!' they chorused.

Minutes later, he'd popped the cork and was filling
their glasses.

Meg helped Dolly to her feet and the three of them
stood together and looked out to sea.

Then Sam raised his glass. 'To Tom Kirby senior,' he
said. 'Dolly's husband and my grandfather—and a brilliant letter writer.'

They clinked glasses and drank.

Smiling down into Meg's eyes, he kissed her and she
tasted of champagne and laughter and love. Then he
added, 'And to Tom Kirby junior, our son and great-
grandson.'

Just then there was a clatter of feet on the stairs and
Tom, his black hair windswept and his blue eyes sparkling, raced ahead of his sisters. 'Are we really having

lasagne and chocolate-layer cake?' he shouted breath-lessly.

The adults laughed. And Sam reached over and wrapped an arm around his son's shoulders. Once more he raised his glass. 'As I was saying, to Tom junior—a kid who, right from when he was born, has always had a great sense of timing.'

Once more they laughed, clinked their glasses, toasted and drank their champagne.

Meg's and Sam's eyes met.

'Oh, oh,' he heard Bella warn Claire. 'They look like they're thinking about kissing again.'

His daughter was a mind-reader.

MILLS & BOON®

Makes any time special™

Mills & Boon publish 29 new titles every month. Select from...

Modern Romance™   Tender Romance™

Sensual Romance™

Medical Romance™   Historical Romance™

MAT2

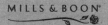

MILLS & BOON

Tender Romance™

THE PROVOCATIVE PROPOSAL – Day Leclaire

Hiring a man wasn't something Tess Lonigan had ever
done before. But in her fast-track career dating was
complicated—far easier to employ a pretend fiancé! Only
Tess had the impression that her appointed candidate
had plans for her himself!

THE BRIDESMAID'S SECRET – Sophie Weston

Handsome millionaire Gil de la Court suspected there
was a lot more to Bella Carew than just a party girl – and
he wanted to know it all! But what if he discovered that
she thought she was in love with another man?

CLAIMING HIS BABY – Rebecca Winters

Dr Raul Cardenas discovered the consequences of their
night of passion before Heather Sanders. He ran a
routine pregnancy test and was amazed at the result –
positive! Raul knew he was the father. This meant he had
two shocking announcements for Heather...

INHERITED: TWINS! – Jessica Hart

Although Outback rancher Nat Masterman is guardian of
eight-month-old twins he doesn't know a thing about
babies—until he meets Prue... She wishes she hadn't told
her family she was bringing home a gorgeous Australian
– there's no such man! At least not until she meets Nat...

On sale 7th September 2001

0801/02

FREE!

2 Books
and a surprise gift!

We would like to take this opportunity to thank you for reading this Mills & Boon® book by offering you the chance to take TWO more specially selected titles from the Tender Romance™ series absolutely FREE! We're also making this offer to introduce you to the benefits of the Reader Service™—

- ★ FREE home delivery
- ★ FREE gifts and competitions
- ★ FREE monthly Newsletter
- ★ Books available before they're in the shops
- ★ Exclusive Reader Service discounts

Accepting these FREE books and gift places you under no obligation to buy; you may cancel at any time, even after receiving your free shipment. Simply complete your details below and return the entire page to the address below. *You don't even need a stamp!*

YES! Please send me 2 free Tender Romance books and a surprise gift. I understand that unless you hear from me, I will receive 4 superb new titles every month for just £2.49 each, postage and packing free. I am under no obligation to purchase any books and may cancel my subscription at any time. The free books and gift will be mine to keep in any case.

N1ZEB

Ms/Mrs/Miss/Mr ....Initials..
BLOCK CAPITALS PLEASE

Surname...

Address...

....

....Postcode ....

Send this whole page to:
UK: The Reader Service, FREEPOST CN81, Croydon, CR9 3WZ
EIRE: The Reader Service, PO Box 4546, Kilcock, County Kildare (stamp required)